EVERY SECRET LEADS TO ANOTHER

# SECRETS *of the* MANOR

Claire's Story, 1910

BY

## ADELE WHITBY

Simon Spotlight

New York  London  Toronto  Sydney  New Delhi

SIMON SPOTLIGHT
An imprint of Simon & Schuster Children's Publishing Division
1230 Avenue of the Americas, New York, New York 10020
This Simon Spotlight paperback edition May 2015
Copyright © 2015 by Simon and Schuster, Inc. Text by Ellie O'Ryan.
Cover illustrations by Francesca Resta. Interior illustrations by Jaime Zollars.
All rights reserved, including the right of reproduction in whole or in part in any
form. SIMON SPOTLIGHT and colophon are registered trademarks of
Simon & Schuster, Inc. For information about special discounts for bulk
purchases, please contact Simon & Schuster Special Sales at 1-866-506-1949 or
business@simonandschuster.com.
Designed by Laura Roode. The text of this book was set in Adobe Caslon Pro.
Manufactured in the United States of America 0415 OFF
2 4 6 8 10 9 7 5 3 1
ISBN 978-1-4814-3992-3 (hc)
ISBN 978-1-4814-3991-6 (pbk)
ISBN 978-1-4814-3993-0 (eBook)
Library of Congress Control Number
2014947119

$C$ome now, my dear Claire," Cousin Colette said. "You must be exhausted from your journey. I'm sure you would appreciate some quiet time to rest in your new room."

I nodded my head in agreement, but to be honest, I didn't feel a bit tired—not one bit! I was far too jumpy and jangly with anticipation, and what I really wanted to do was explore every inch of Rousseau Manor's grand house and grounds. I wanted to spend hours getting to know my cousins Henri and Colette Rousseau, who would be my guardians from now on. Most of all, I wanted to do everything I could to make this unfamiliar place feel like home—and to make these strangers feel like family.

The best way to do that, it seemed, was to do exactly what my new guardians asked of me. That's why I didn't resist when Cousin Colette and Cousin Henri led me past the receiving line of servants and through the entrance of Rousseau Manor. But I did turn my head around to peek behind me one more time. The girl near the end of the line was still standing there, watching me—Camille, she was called—and as soon as our eyes met, she smiled. I smiled back as I waved at her over my shoulder. We were almost the exact same height, which made me think Camille was nearly twelve years old, like me. She was the very first person my age I'd met since I had arrived in Paris. There was something about her—a spark of kindness, I think, or maybe it was the friendly way her face crinkled up when she smiled—that made me wish we could be friends. But Camille was a servant here, and I had no idea when I'd see her again.

"This way, Claire." Cousin Colette's voice interrupted my thoughts. I hurried to catch up, pausing for only a minute to marvel at the grand entryway of Rousseau Manor, where gold trim made the walls and ceiling gleam. I wished I could've stopped to stare at *everything*—Rousseau Manor was even grander than I had imagined it would be.

"Wait," I said suddenly. "Where are my trunks?"

"Ah, of course," Cousin Colette replied. "After you've rested, I'll have the footmen bring them up. We will hire a lady's maid for you in due course, but Henri and I thought you should have a say in whom we choose. So until then our head housemaid, Bernadette, will attend to you. I'll see to it that she unpacks your trunk and organizes your belongings while we dine."

"No!" I said suddenly. I didn't want to be disagreeable, but . . .

Cousin Colette looked at me in surprise. I took a deep breath and tried again. "If it's not too much inconvenience, I'd like to unpack myself—as soon as possible."

"Yes, of course, my dear," Cousin Colette said. "Whatever you desire."

She stepped over to the butler for a brief word and then returned to my side. "We've chosen a room on the second floor of the East Wing for you," she said as we climbed the spiral staircase. "I hope that you'll find the room suitable. With the eastern exposure, you'll have a lovely view of the sunrise each morning. Of course, you may not be an early riser, but I can assure you the curtains are velvet and very thick; they'll be sure to block out the light. And if there is anything about the decor you'd like to change, you need only say the word. . . ."

Cousin Colette's voice trailed off as she reached out to open the door. I caught a quick glimpse of a canopy bed with billowing white curtains, blue velvet drapes, and a plush rug to match, but I didn't need to see my new room to express my gratitude.

"It's perfect," I said. "Thank you."

A relieved smile washed over Cousin Colette's face, and for the first time I wondered if she felt as nervous as I did. She squeezed my hand as the footmen arrived, bearing my trunks.

"Where would you like them, Mademoiselle Claire?" the taller one asked.

"Oh, anywhere is fine," I said. "Perhaps by the window?" It had a deep window seat that was crowded with velvet pillows; I could already tell that I would spend many happy hours there, basking in the morning sun as I read my favorite books.

"You mustn't worry about the unpacking," Cousin Henri said. "The entire staff here is at your service and will be more than happy to assist you in any way they can."

"Thank you," I repeated. Perhaps I should've told them that unpacking as quickly as possible was all part of my plan to make Rousseau Manor feel like home. But I didn't quite know how to say it, so we stood together in an uncomfortable silence, the way strangers might stand together on the platform as they await the next train.

Suddenly, Cousin Colette leaned forward to embrace me. "We are so glad you have come to Rousseau Manor," she whispered near my ear, "though we wish it had happened under different circumstances."

Tears pricked at my eyes then, but I tried to blink them away. There would be no melancholy or weepy moments for me. No, I would be happy and cheerful and a joy to have at Rousseau Manor. That was the vow I had made on the voyage from America. After all, that's what Mother and Father would've wanted me to do.

But were those tears shining in Cousin Colette's eyes as well? I knew what it looked like when adults were trying not to cry in front of me. I'd seen it quite a bit in the last few weeks.

"We'll send Bernadette in later on to help you dress for dinner," she finished.

Cousin Henri smiled winningly at me before he escorted Cousin Colette from the room.

And then I was all alone for perhaps the first time since the accident that had killed my parents and left me an orphan. Since that terrible night, everyone had been so tremendously *kind* to me . . . and the people of Rousseau Manor were no exception.

I went straight to my trunk and unlatched the strong brass buckles. I didn't even notice how anxious I was until I eased open the lid, waiting to see if the precious contents had survived the rough crossing overseas. My hands were trembling a bit as I unwrapped the bundles—the big one first. I opened the sturdy case and breathed a sigh of relief to discover that Father's beautiful violin was in perfect condition, looking just as it had the very last time he had played for me. The polished wood gleamed in a beam of sunlight as I lightly rested my fingers on the taut strings. After I unpacked the bow, perhaps I could play a little. If I closed my eyes, it might even feel as if Father was playing for me once more.

I reached for the second bundle, which was much smaller and lighter. Inside the silk handkerchief, I found them: Mother's favorite pair of gloves and a small cameo brooch that she always wore pinned to the front of her dress.

I slipped my hands into the gloves, knowing that hers were the last hands to wear them. They even smelled like her delicate perfume. A wide smile filled my face; anywhere would feel like home with these special reminders of Mother and Father by my side.

I reached into the trunk for Father's bow and found something surprising instead:

A letter.

*I don't remember any letters in here when the maids helped me pack my trunk,* I thought as a confused frown spread across my face. But sure enough, my name was written on the front in perfect, elegant script. I opened the envelope and began to read.

*Dear Claire,*

*As I write this letter on the eve of your departure, there is much hope swirling through my heart: that you will have a*

pleasant journey; that you will find France to be as wonderful and welcoming as I have during my visits; that you will feel quite at home the moment you arrive at Rousseau Manor; and, most of all, that the grief you feel for your parents will be replaced by only the sweetest memories of them.

You know, of course, that your mother was a dear friend, and her untimely passing is a great injustice that no one who loved her should have to bear. And yet I have found that your presence here at Vandermeer Manor has done wonders to soothe my grief. It is a testament to your character, Claire, that even in the face of such tragedy, you are compassionate and kind. More than once I have observed you at play with Kate and little Alfie and thought about how proud

your parents would be of your strength and
resiliency.

Knowing this, I am confident that
you will find a warm welcome at Rousseau
Manor and soon feel very much at home
there. I met Henri and Colette many years
ago and found them to be a charming couple
with generous, giving hearts. And when you
find yourself on American shores once more, I
do hope you will visit us here at Vandermeer
Manor. We will always have a room ready for
you, and I look forward to seeing your sweet
face at my table once more.

With my fondest regards,

Mrs. Katherine Vandermeer

I read the letter twice more before I finally returned
it to its envelope. It was just like dear, sweet Mrs.
Vandermeer, Kate and Alfie's great-grandmother, to

write something so kind and heartening, then slip it into my trunk so that I should discover it right when I might need some reassurance! Reading her words made me wish, for the briefest moment, that I was still at Vandermeer Manor, listening to Kate practice her reading or helping Alfie arrange his toy soldiers. A wave of homesickness washed over me as I sat beside my trunk, all alone in a strange land.

A sudden knock at the door interrupted my thoughts.

"Come in," I said, scrambling to my feet as I hurried to take off Mother's gloves. I'd thought it would be Cousin Colette, or perhaps a housemaid to help me unpack, but instead it was the girl I'd met in the receiving line. Camille.

"Pardon the interruption, Mademoiselle Claire," she said right away, ducking into a curtsy as she balanced a heavy tray, "but we thought that you might be in need of some refreshments."

"What's this?" I cried as I hurried across the room. The tray was so laden with treats that I marveled at Camille's ability to carry it, let alone curtsy without spilling a single thing. There were slices of crusty bread and a wedge of creamy cheese; a basket filled to the brim with cookies; a platter of pastries; a bowl of chocolate-covered strawberries; and a tall glass of milk. There was even a vase with a large, fragrant white flower.

"How beautiful!" I gasped as I leaned down to sniff it. I didn't remember the name of the flower, but its scent reminded me of Mother. She'd grown flowers like this in one of our gardens.

"Where did you get this?" I asked Camille, hardly daring to hope that other flowers like this one might grow somewhere on the grounds of Rousseau Manor.

"It comes from the flower garden," she told me. "Tomorrow, if you'd like, I would be happy to give you a tour of the house and grounds."

"Would you really?" I asked in excitement. "That would be wonderful. Thank you!"

"It would be my pleasure, Mademoiselle Claire. I will come to your room after breakfast."

"Please, you really must call me Claire," I told her.

Camille looked a bit worried. "Are you—are you sure?" she asked. "It seems so informal . . . disrespectful, almost. . . ."

"Nonsense!" I replied. Then, impulsively, I gestured toward the window seat. "Come. You must join me. I can't eat *all* of this by myself!"

Camille glanced over her shoulder. "I should get back," she said. But when Camille looked at me again, something in her face changed. "But perhaps I can spare a few minutes."

I closed the lid of my trunk so that it became a table for us. "What should I try first?" I asked.

Camille looked at the tray thoughtfully. "Well, these are my favorites," she said, pointing at a puffed-up ball of pastry with a thin glaze of chocolate on top. "They're called profiteroles, and they're filled with custard."

"Mmm," I said as I reached for one and took a bite. "Delicious!"

Camille smiled so proudly that I wondered if she had made them. I was about to ask when she suddenly said, "A violin!"

"It belonged to my father," I explained.

A look of understanding flashed through Camille's eyes. "What a special thing to have," she said as she squeezed my hand. "My papa died when I was five years old, and Mama let me keep one of his red hand-kerchiefs. I still have it."

*She knows,* I thought as I smiled gratefully at Camille. *She knows what this feels like.*

"Do you play?" she continued.

"Oh, no," I said, shaking my head. "Well, a little, I suppose. But badly—very badly. I only wish I had inherited my father's musical gifts!"

Camille giggled. "I feel the same way about my mother's culinary skills," she confided. "She's a genius in the kitchen, but I'm a laughingstock, an absolute disaster!"

She turned away briefly to glance at the clock hanging on the wall.

"I really must go, I'm afraid," she said as she rose. "I need to watch Baby Sophie while her mother prepares the servants' meal."

I rose with her. "Thank you for the visit and the refreshments," I replied, though what I wanted to say was, *I do wish you could stay!*

After Camille took her leave, my new room seemed so much quieter and lonesome. *Perhaps I should've insisted that she stay,* I thought. But of course I would never do such a thing—not when she had responsibilities to attend to. It would be unfair to put her in such a position.

*There's no reason I can't start exploring the gardens myself,* I decided. I put on my favorite hat, the one with embroidered cherries scattered around the brim, and reached for my smart spring coat. Just before I left my room, I decided to take Father's violin with me. He always loved to play outdoors on a bright spring day or a warm summer evening. Perhaps I would grow to love it too.

I made my way downstairs and out the grand double doors, wondering if I'd see Cousin Colette or Cousin Henri and need to explain why I was wandering about with a violin case tucked under my arm. The only people I saw, though, were a few housemaids, who looked at me curiously before ducking into deep curtsies. I smiled broadly at them as I tried to remember their names. I'd met so many new people that everything was a blur!

Outside, I followed a stone path around the back of the house, where the gardens stretched out like a beautiful patchwork quilt. A tall hedge lined the path, which twisted and turned across the property. I followed it until I came to a lovely little garden that was positively bursting with flowers in bloom, including the ones that Mother used to grow! How I wished I could remember the name of those flowers.

There was a white marble bench in the middle of the garden, so I sat on it while I removed Father's violin from the case and added a little extra rosin to the bow. Then, after carefully positioning my chin on the leather chin rest, I began to play his favorite song from memory. But the notes sounded all wrong! It was no secret that I was a poor excuse for a musician, especially compared to Father; I stopped playing after a screechy note that was off-tempo besides. The last thing I wanted to do was butcher Father's favorite song.

Then I tried my hand at a simpler tune. It wasn't anything special, but I played it passably well. I closed my eyes as I imagined what he would say if he could hear my playing: "Better. Better! I can tell you've been practicing!" Even though we both knew that I hadn't been—not as much as I should've, anyway.

The memory brought a smile to my face, but it

lasted only a moment before it faded. I had the strangest sense . . . a creeping feeling that started at the base of my head before crawling down my spine. It felt like someone was *watching* me.

I opened my eyes. "Who's there?" I called out loudly. Half the battle in facing one's fears was to face them head-on, or at least, that's what Mother always used to tell me. So I was pleasantly surprised by how steady my voice sounded.

I listened carefully but heard no reply. I had no choice but to conclude that I was alone in the little garden: completely, totally, and utterly alone.

Yet the feeling persisted; if anything, it grew stronger, until I was as certain as I could be that no matter what my eyes told me, I was not by myself after all.

I didn't dare hope that I might be feeling the presence of my dear father visiting me from the world beyond. I would be twelve years old in a few months, and everyone knew that twelve was way too grown-up to believe in specters and haunts from beyond the grave.

Even though I would've given anything—*anything*—for one more afternoon with my parents.

I took a deep breath and nestled Father's violin under my chin once more. Then, taking extra care to hold the bow just so and to place my fingers firmly against the strings, I again attempted to play Father's favorite song . . . just in case.

I couldn't say how much time passed as I lingered in the garden, surrounded by Mother's favorite blooms while I played Father's violin. But by the time I returned to my room, Bernadette—the head housemaid who would serve as my lady's maid until one was hired—was waiting for me. She curtsied as soon as I entered.

"Good afternoon, Mademoiselle Claire," she said. "I apologize for the intrusion. I have come to help you dress for dinner."

"Goodness!" I cried, searching for the clock before I remembered that it was on the wall. "Is it time already?"

"Usually, Madame Colette and Monsieur Henri eat at half-past eight," she replied. "But Madame thought you might be accustomed to eating earlier, so she requested that dinner be served no later than six o'clock."

"How very kind of her," I said. "At home ... I mean to say, in America, we would eat at eight o'clock."

"You must tell Madame that at dinner," Bernadette said. "Now, have you given any thought to what you might like to wear this evening? I can tell you that dinner at Rousseau Manor is a very formal affair."

"I suppose my violet silk might be best," I said thoughtfully. "But I'm sure it's terribly wrinkled from the journey."

"If it please you, Mademoiselle Claire, I took the liberty of bringing your dinner dresses to the laundry this afternoon," Bernadette replied. "They are pressed and hanging in the wardrobe."

I peeked inside the tall mahogany wardrobe and found my dresses hanging there, just the way Laura used to hang them back home. "Thank you, Bernadette," I said. "That was very considerate of you."

"Not at all, mademoiselle."

Bernadette worked swiftly to dress me in the violet silk. It was a beautiful gown, but it had dozens of finicky pearl buttons down the back that troubled Bernadette as she attempted to fasten them.

"I apologize, Mademoiselle Claire," she said.

19

"There's no need," I replied at once. "You're not the first to struggle with them!"

Luckily, my hair was much easier to fix. Just a few months ago, Mother had agreed to let me cut it in a short bob that curled around my ears. It took only a few strokes of the hairbrush and a handful of pins to have it looking stylish.

"There!" Bernadette said as she placed the last pin in my hair. "Is there anything else you'd like?"

"Just one thing," I told her as I reached for Mother's gloves. The satin was cool and smooth as I pulled them over my hands. If Bernadette noticed that they were still a tad too big, she didn't mention it.

"I'll show you to the drawing room, if you'd like," she offered. "That's where the Rousseaus gather before they take their seats in the dining room."

"Please," I said gratefully. Since I hadn't had a proper tour of Rousseau Manor yet, the endless corridors seemed like a hopelessly complicated maze.

Bernadette smiled kindly. "You'll find everything in no time," she said, as if she could read my thoughts.

Just outside the drawing room, I fidgeted with my dress—straightening the shoulders, smoothing the skirt. I pulled up my loose gloves one more time and willed them to stay put.

I took a deep breath.

Then I stepped through the doorway.

Cousin Henri and Cousin Colette were on their feet at once.

"Ahh, here she is!" announced Cousin Henri.

"You look lovely, Claire," Cousin Colette said as she approached me. I thought at first that she was going to hug me, but instead her hands fluttered by my shoulders as if, at the last moment, she'd lost her nerve and decided to pat my arm instead.

"I trust you had a pleasant afternoon," she continued. "Did you rest?"

"I—I took the air," I said, not wanting to lie. "The gardens are most pleasant."

"Yes," Cousin Henri said. "Especially this time of year."

Silence descended over us then, and I wondered if my cousins were having as much difficulty thinking of something to say as I was.

Finally, Cousin Henri cleared his throat. "Shall we?" he asked, offering his left arm to Cousin Colette and his right arm to me. "I am a lucky man to dine with two such beautiful ladies tonight!"

In the dining room, Cousin Colette sat at one end of the table while Cousin Henri took his place at the other end. There was a third place set in the center, so I sat there. *Just the three of us, I suppose,* I thought. How different it was from our table in America, which was always crowded with Mother and Father's friends!

I took a sip of water as the footmen arrived, bearing the first course—bowls of creamy potato-and-leek vichyssoise soup.

"There will be much to attend to in the coming weeks," Cousin Colette said. "You and I shall sit together in the parlor, and you will tell me all your favorite dishes so that our cook, Mrs. Plourde, can add them to the menu. I'll make sure they're in frequent rotation."

"Thank you," I replied. "But please, I don't want anyone to go to any trouble on my account. I'm just grateful to be here."

Cousin Colette's smile wavered, and I wondered if I'd said the wrong thing. I patted my lips with my napkin to hide my self-consciousness. Everyone had told me that the Rousseaus were charming and friendly, and yet we could hardly carry on a conversation for more than a sentence or two. Was there something wrong with me? Perhaps they really didn't want to be my guardians after all. Perhaps they would've preferred it if I'd stayed in America.

"Lessons," Cousin Henri spoke up suddenly. "We will make arrangements for you to continue with your lessons. Composition, language, arithmetic . . ."

"I trust, in the family tradition, that you were receiving training in the arts as well?" Cousin Colette inquired. "Painting, drawing, music?"

"Yes, all three," I replied. "Though I am considerably less skilled in some fields than others. You may find it useful to plug your ears to protect them during my music lessons."

I thought a little joke would make us all feel more comfortable, but I was the only one who laughed.

*It's hopeless!* I thought in frustration as the next course arrived. Perhaps Cousin Colette was right and I should've spent the afternoon resting; the rigors of dinner conversation with my guardians felt like more than I could handle.

*Well,* I thought, *at least I can enjoy this wonderful meal.* Father had often told me that the food in France was better than anywhere else in the world. "Someday we'll take you, *ma chérie*," he would say, using his special endearment for me. "And you can eat food the way I ate it growing up in France. The way it was meant to be prepared." He would've loved every dish that the footmen served, I was sure. The chicken and mushrooms were so delicious that I wished I could've licked the plate! Remembering the delightful profiteroles that Camille had brought me that afternoon made me look forward to dessert, even though I was soon so full that I was worried I wouldn't be able to eat a single bite more. But when the footmen brought in a dessert I'd never seen before, I knew I'd have to try it—at least a tiny taste!

"What's this called?" I asked as the footman placed a slice before me.

"Mille-feuille," Cousin Henri replied. "It's a very delicate kind of pastry layered with sweet cream. Go on—taste it!"

I brought the fork to my mouth. The pastry seemed to melt into nothingness on my tongue, while the creamy filling was rich and sweet.

"That's amazing!" I cried, before I remembered the proper, quiet manners I should've used at the table. But Cousin Henri and Cousin Colette didn't seem to disapprove of my outburst. In fact, Cousin Henri seemed almost delighted by it.

"Aha!" He laughed. "You see, Colette, I am no longer the only one in this house who can appreciate a fine dessert!"

Cousin Colette shook her head in mock exasperation, but the smile on her face gave her away. "Henri, I am surprised that you greet this news with such enthusiasm," she chided him. "I would've thought that you would prefer to have all the desserts for yourself."

Then Cousin Colette turned to me. "If you're partial to sweets, Claire, you will be very happy here," she said. "We are fortunate to employ the best pastry chef in all of France, Marie LeClerc. You met her this afternoon, along with her daughter, Camille."

"Oh, yes, Camille!" I exclaimed as I figured out the connection. "She came to my room this afternoon with a tray full of sweets, and she never once mentioned that her mother had made them! I was very grateful to her, as I found I was hungrier than I expected. She is very kind, isn't she? We had a very nice little chat, and I was so glad for her visit."

I smiled brightly as I waited for a response . . . but no one said anything. Instead—and I wish I could say that this was a figment of my imagination, but I'm certain that I saw it—I caught a strange look pass between my cousins. They seemed concerned—almost *worried*—by what I had said. I looked down at my plate, having suddenly lost my appetite, and idly pushed a strawberry around with my fork. Was it something I'd said? Something I'd done?

Why did Cousin Henri and Cousin Colette keep acting so oddly?

*I hope that I haven't gotten Camille into trouble,* I fretted. I didn't *think* that she'd done anything wrong, but perhaps the rules were different here in France. Mrs. Vandermeer had warned me that I might find more formality at a French estate than I was accustomed to in America.

But wouldn't Camille have warned me not to say anything, if that were the case?

If the mere mention of Camille could upset my

cousins like that, then I would take care not to speak her name unless it was essential. Suddenly, I found myself looking forward with even greater anticipation to the tour Camille had promised me. Camille was the friendliest person I'd met since I set foot in France— and I was in dire need of a friend.

I didn't want to do anything that might jeopardize that.

After breakfast the next morning, I returned to my room to wait for Camille. A few moments later, I heard a tap on the door.

"Hello!" I cried happily.

"Good morning," she replied with a grin. "Is now still a convenient time for your tour?"

"Certainly! I've been looking forward to it," I said. "Will we go outside first? Do I need my hat?"

"Whatever you prefer, of course," she said at once.

I thought for a moment. "Let's start inside, and if there's still time before lunch, we can get our hats and go outside as well. If *you* have the time, I should say. I seem to have nothing *but* free time. At least, until my lessons begin."

Camille brightened. "I wonder if we'll have the same tutor," she said. Then she shook her head. "Oh, of *course* not. What was I thinking? I'm sure you'll—"

"You have lessons?" I exclaimed. The thought had never occurred to me, perhaps because there were no young servants at the American Rousseau Manor.

"Thanks to the Rousseaus' generosity," she said, blushing a bit. "I am very grateful to them."

"In that case, I do hope we will share a tutor," I said. "It would be such fun! Like a little school!"

Then I remembered what had happened at dinner last night, which dampened my enthusiasm. Had Camille gotten in trouble? Would she even tell me if she had?

There was only one way to know for sure.

"At dinner with Cousins Henri and Colette last night . . . ," I began.

Camille waited for me to continue, but I wasn't quite sure what to say—or how to say it.

"I . . . Well, your mother's dessert was very good," I stammered. "Delicious, really!"

Camille smiled. "Excellent! She'll be very glad to hear it."

"And, well, I might have mentioned that you brought some treats to my room in the afternoon," I continued awkwardly. "I hope that was all right."

For a moment Camille looked confused. "I'm sure it was fine," she replied. "As long as I wasn't disturbing you. And should I ever do that, you must only say the word—"

I shook my head. "Oh, no. You wouldn't be disturbing me," I told her. It didn't seem that she'd gotten in trouble for anything I'd said at the table, which filled me with relief but also curiosity. If Camille hadn't been breaking the rules, then why had Cousin Henri and Cousin Colette reacted like that?

"Shall we begin the tour?" Camille asked. We walked into the hallway, where she gestured at the ceiling. "The third floor is the servants' quarters. Very dull, actually—just a lot of little rooms—so we can skip it."

I looked around the hall. "I didn't realize there was a third floor," I replied.

"There's a hidden staircase behind that door," Camille told me as she pointed to the end of the hall. "That servants' staircase is actually the only way to get to the third floor."

I looked at the dark brown door with interest. The door seemed entirely ordinary, as though it led to a normal room. "I never would've guessed! There are servants' staircases at Vandermeer Manor but not at the American Rousseau Manor."

"Servants' staircases and corridors snake all around within the walls of Rousseau Manor," Camille explained. "The family never has to see us as we go about our work. Of course, the Rousseaus aren't like that, not at all. They don't mind if we use the regular halls and stairs if it's more convenient."

I smiled. That sounded like the sort of approach Mother and Father would have had, and it made me feel a bit more at home.

"This part of the second floor contains mostly guest rooms," Camille continued. She opened each door, one at a time, so that I could peek inside it. "The peach room . . . the gold room . . . the green room . . . the gray room . . ."

There was one door, I noticed, that Camille swiftly and deliberately walked past.

"What's in there?" I asked.

"That?" she said quickly—too quickly. "Oh, that

room's nothing, but if you'd like to go to the West Wing now. That's where my mother and I live—"

My curiosity was piqued. I slipped over to the door and reached for the cold brass knob.

"Wait—don't—"

It was too late, though. Because just as the words left Camille's mouth, the door swung open.

$C$ome on," I said to Camille as I stepped over the threshold. She followed me without saying a word, then rushed to close the door behind us.

What I found when I opened the door was hardly the shocking surprise I'd expected. It was, after all, just a room—a very pretty and well-appointed room, with rosebuds on the wallpaper and a canopy bed with pink velvet drapes. But apart from that, there was nothing unusual about it. I couldn't imagine why Camille had been so eager to skip over it.

I walked farther into the room, marveling at all the beautiful dolls in the curio cabinet and a darling menagerie of wind-up animals. There was a vanity full of atomizers and shelves that were positively crammed with books. In short, the room was perfect.

"What a darling room," I said.

Camille's worried expression melted away as

a beaming smile crossed her face. She clasped her hands together. "I was hoping you would like it!" she exclaimed. "I'm so glad to hear you say that!"

"And there's a balcony," I said. "Let's take in the view."

"Oh, no," Camille replied at once. "We mustn't do that. Someone might see us. We're not even supposed to *be* in here. It's forbidden."

Now I was *really* curious about this room, which was so lovely and yet so mysterious at the same time. "Well, we could stand to the side of the doors and peek around the curtains, couldn't we?" I suggested. "I don't think anyone would see us if we did that."

Camille pursed her lips. "I suppose that would be all right," she said. "But just for a moment or two."

I carefully reached out and pulled back just the edge of the sheer white curtains. Across from me, Camille did the same. A breathtaking view of the estate was revealed to us; I could see an apple orchard in full bloom; fountains bubbling merrily; and a very unusual garden full of large, overgrown bushes. The grounds-keeper was working busily in it.

"What's that, over there?" I asked, craning my

neck as I tried to get a better look.

"Those are the topiary gardens," Camille explained. "The new groundskeeper, Phillipe, and his son, Alexandre, are working to restore them. Each bush will be clipped and shaped into a different animal."

"How lovely," I said. "One could sit out on the balcony every day and watch the transformation take place."

That's when a splendid idea occurred to me. "I'm going to ask Cousin Colette if I might move into this room," I announced. "It's far too special to stay closed up all the time."

Camille immediately went pale. "No, no, no!" she said. "No, you mustn't, Claire! Monsieur Henri forbade anyone from setting foot in this room ever again."

"But *why*?" I asked incredulously. "Why on earth would he want that, when the room is so prettily arranged, as if it's just waiting for a girl to move in?"

Camille's eyes darted toward the door. When she was assured that it was still shut tight, she gestured me over to a bench at the foot of the bed. "I probably shouldn't even tell you this," she began in a low voice that immediately captured my interest. I sat up straight, filled with anticipation for the secret that she was about to reveal.

"Madame Colette and Monsieur Henri had a daughter, and this was her room," continued Camille. "Her name was Mademoiselle Claudia, and when she was of age she fell in love with a dashing young man from Germany—against their wishes. They had a terrible fight about it. Then Mademoiselle Claudia ran away with her sweetheart in the dark of night."

"No," I breathed, shocked by the tale. "I had no idea. Then what happened?"

"All I know for certain is that Mademoiselle Claudia died," Camille said.

"But there must be more to the story," I insisted. I always loved a good mystery. And this one was full of romance as well. "Where did she go when she left Rousseau Manor? Did she marry her sweetheart? Did she ever make amends with her parents?"

Camille looked like there was something she wanted to say.

"There *is* more to the story!" I cried. "Oh, do tell, Camille. You can trust me. I swear it."

"There is a diary," she whispered. "Mademoiselle

Claudia's diary. I found it among her old books, but I haven't read it. I hid it here for safekeeping."

"You mean to say that it's here? Right here, in this very room?" I asked.

Camille nodded.

"Why, I think we ought to read it—don't you?" I said.

"I don't know," she said slowly. "It doesn't seem right."

"But think of it this way," I pressed. "If we read it and find out more about Cousin Claudia, we'll be able to avoid accidentally upsetting Cousin Colette and Cousin Henri."

"That's a good point," Camille acknowledged. "But I still don't think it would be right. . . . At least, it wouldn't be right for *me* to read it. You're family; Mademoiselle Claudia was your cousin. It's different."

I waved my hand in the air. "Nonsense. That doesn't matter at all. Come; we'll read it together and take a vow of secrecy never to reveal the contents to anyone!"

"All right," Camille finally agreed. "If you're sure."

"Positive," I replied.

Camille lifted the quilted silk blanket and rummaged around under the mattress until, at last, she withdrew a small leather book. My breath caught in my throat; I couldn't *wait* to find out what secrets Cousin Claudia had committed to its pages, but there was something important that we had to do first.

I held the diary in my open palm, then placed Camille's hand on top of it. "I vow to keep this diary secret," I said in my most serious voice.

"I vow to keep this diary secret," Camille repeated.

Then we opened the book, leaned our heads together, and began to read.

*29 April 1898*

*To this blank book, I will commit the best memories of my life: the love-filled days of my marriage to H—.*

*I am recently returned to my childhood home, grief-stricken at the untimely passing of H—. There are moments that hearten me: Mama and Papa have welcomed me home with open arms,*

37

and in my sorrow there is no place I'd rather be than here, with them. I have tried to apologize for disappearing as I did, but they won't hear it. Mama says that we will just pretend that none of it happened, but how could I ever do such a thing? My heart cannot tell such a lie, and I wouldn't dream of dishonoring my husband's memory or our love.

"I didn't know that Mademoiselle—I mean Madame—Claudia got married!" Camille exclaimed. "Or that her husband died. That's so sad. Poor Madame Claudia."

"She came home, though," I pointed out. "She reconciled with her parents. They made amends before her death." I quickly turned the page and passed the book to Camille. "Here. You read the next one aloud."

30 *April* 1898

When H— asked for my hand in marriage this past January, I already knew just what sort of gown I wanted to wear to our wedding! But Papa said no—no! With that one simple word, all my hopes and dreams for a formal wedding were dashed. But there was one dream that nothing could destroy: marrying my H—. Is it any wonder I left for Alsace that very night? His parents were none too happy when H— brought me home from the train station, but by then it was too late: We had been wed in the village that very day.

I grinned at Camille. "I think I would've done the very same thing," I confided.

This time, Camille turned the page and passed the book to me. I took a deep breath and began to read aloud.

15 May 1898

There is no one in the world who knows the secret I am about to commit to these pages. I had intended this book to chronicle all the sweet memories of *courtship and marriage to H—. But instead of looking to the past, I shall now dedicate these pages to the future. For the future is suddenly brighter and more beautiful than it has ever been before: I am going to be a mother!*

Camille and I gasped as we looked at each other with wide eyes.

"A mother!" I shrieked, completely forgetting to be quiet. "Cousin Claudia was going to have a baby!"

Camille was clearly as astonished as I was, but she had the good sense to put a finger to her lips, reminding me to hush. I stopped speaking immediately . . . just in time to hear an unusual sound—a muted crash, as though someone had dropped something on the plush carpet.

It came from the hall.

From right outside the door.

Which meant that whoever had dropped it must have heard every word I'd said.

Camille grabbed my arm in alarm. I strained my ears in the silence, trying to hear something—anything—that would tell me if the person was still outside the room.

Nothing.

Then, slowly, the doorknob began to turn.

*Someone's coming in!* I thought in a wild panic.

Camille, fortunately, kept her wits about her. She flew across the room and opened a closet door—only it wasn't a closet at all, but a small room. No, it was a passageway. That's when I realized that Camille had figured out a way for us to escape: through the servants' entrance!

I shoved Cousin Claudia's diary in a drawer and rushed after Camille. Quick as a wink, we were in the dim, dusty passage, running as fast as we dared. When Camille stopped abruptly, I almost ran into her, but caught myself just in time. She pressed her ear against a door, listening carefully, before she pushed it open. I followed her, only to realize that we were back in the hallway, not far from my own room.

And we weren't alone.

"Alexandre!" Camille exclaimed suddenly, her face blushing ever so slightly. "What are—"

I immediately recognized the boy, whom I'd met the day before. He was the groundskeeper's son. His tousled, brown hair and bright green eyes were unforgettable.

Alexandre nodded his head at us, but he wouldn't meet my eye. "Good day, Mademoiselle Claire. Good day, Camille," he mumbled, before turning around and hurrying down the hall in the opposite direction. I watched him go, feeling more confused than ever.

Camille was watching him with a puzzled look on her face too. "I've never seen Alexandre on the second floor before," she said in a low voice. "He should be outside, working in the garden with his father."

"Do you think *he's* the one who heard us?" I asked eagerly. I didn't know Alexandre at all, but surely that would be better than Cousin Henri or Cousin Colette knowing what we'd been up to.

"I don't—," Camille began. Then she caught herself. "Perhaps we should discuss it in your room."

"Of course," I said right away as I reached for the doorknob. Once we were safely inside, I closed the door behind us and breathed a sigh of relief. "So who do you think was outside Claudia's room?" I asked. "Alexandre?"

Camille shook her head. "Probably not. It would've taken him a lot longer to get here without using the shortcut through the servants' passage."

"Then who?"

"It could've been anyone, really," she mused. "A housemaid or a footman or . . ."

"Cousin Henri or Cousin Colette?"

"Perhaps. But I doubt it. I think they would've stormed into the room if they'd heard us," Camille replied. But I noticed that she looked terribly worried once more.

"Don't fret," I said, patting her arm reassuringly. "Even *if* they learned we were in the room, I'll take all the blame. It was my idea to go inside it, after all."

"You don't have to do that," she said.

"Why wouldn't I? It's the truth," I said. "Now, what we've got to do is figure out a way to get that diary."

Camille's eyes widened. "No. We mustn't! It isn't worth the risk!"

"But I've got to find out more," I told her. "Don't you want to learn all about Cousin Claudia's dear little baby?"

"I suppose . . . ," Camille said. "But what if someone discovers us?"

I made up my mind in an instant. "You needn't worry about that," I told her as I rose to my feet.

Camille scrambled up, too. "Wait!" she exclaimed. "Where are you going?"

"I'll go back to Cousin Claudia's room on my own," I told her. "That way, if I'm discovered, I can feign innocence, and no one will be the wiser."

Camille opened her mouth, but I kept talking before she could say a word. "You wait here, and I'll be right back," I promised.

Before Camille could object, I scurried into the hallway and walked swiftly with my head high and my shoulders set with determination. It took only a few moments before I found myself outside Claudia's room.

I glanced quickly to my left, then my right.

The hall was empty.

In a flash, I was inside Claudia's room with the door safely shut behind me. To my relief, there was no one in Claudia's room either. It wasn't until that moment that I realized I'd been holding my breath. I exhaled deeply as I crossed the room to the bureau. From here, everything would be easy: Get the diary, go back into the hallway, and return to my room, where Camille and I would surely read every last word before sundown.

There was just one problem.

The diary was gone.

My face fell into a frown. I *clearly* remembered placing the diary in this drawer ... or was I mistaken? Had I hidden it in another drawer, and in all the excitement forgotten which one?

Well, that riddle would be easy enough to solve. All I would need to do is search each drawer. Three drawers on the left, three drawers on the right, two across the top. I opened each and every one.

Yet the diary was nowhere to be found.

*This can't be right,* I thought as I stared into the empty drawers. I was certain—absolutely certain, without a single doubt—that I'd hidden Claudia's diary in the bureau. There was only one possible explanation for the diary's disappearance.

Whoever had been listening at the door—whoever had heard Camille and me exclaim over the revelation in Claudia's diary—must have taken it.

*I've got to tell Camille,* I thought.

I was in such a state that I burst out of the room without bothering to check if there was anyone in the hall; lucky for me, it was still empty. I must've sounded like a herd of thundering elephants as I charged back to my own room, where I found Camille pacing nervously.

"Did anyone see you? Did you get it?" she cried.

I shook my head. "It's gone," I said breathlessly. "Gone!"

"Gone?" she repeated. "What—how—?"

"Someone must've taken it," I continued, resting my hand over my pounding heart. "After we left through the servants' passage—whoever was listening went into the room and took it—"

"I can't believe it!" Camille said.

"We'll find it," I promised her, but even as the words left my mouth, doubt flickered in my heart. Rousseau Manor was very large, and the diary was very small. It could be anywhere. And I had a sinking suspicion that the person who had it would take pains to make sure it stayed hidden this time.

"Come. Tell me where you first found it," I said. "That's where we should begin our search."

Camille looked troubled. "In the basement . . . ," she began.

"Excellent!" I cried. "We'll go there straightaway."

"I can't," she said quickly. "I've got to watch little Sophie."

"Oh, of course," I replied. "Well, afterward, then."

I thought the matter would be settled, but Camille shook her head. "No, you don't understand," she said, staring at the floor. "I'm not supposed to go to the basement."

I thought for a moment. "But you *are* supposed to help me when I'm in need," I said finally. "And I'm in need of someone to show me to the basement."

Camille tried to smile, but she still looked concerned. "I really shouldn't."

"Nonsense," I told her. "We're just going to look for Claudia's diary. We should search the basement tonight after dinner. There will probably be fewer interruptions then, anyway. And if everyone else in the house is asleep, then there's no reason to be afraid that we'll be discovered."

Camille was slow to answer, so I pressed on. "Please, Camille," I told her. "I need you. I don't know the first thing about Rousseau Manor. I probably couldn't even find my way to the basement without your help!"

"All right," she finally gave in. "If you think it's best."

I nodded firmly, attempting to convince myself and Camille at the same time. *Madame Colette told me to make myself at home here,* I remembered.

Surely that would include the basement, too.

Later that evening, after I bade Cousin Colette and Cousin Henri good night, I dismissed Bernadette, assuring her that I could change into my nightdress on my own. I climbed into bed fully clothed, pulling the blankets up to my chin in the darkness. I listened to the sounds of Rousseau Manor settling for the night: footmen shuttering the windows and housemaids chatting quietly as they climbed the stairs to the servants' quarters. At last the house was still.

I slipped out of bed and listened by my door for another moment or two, but I heard nothing. Satisfied that everyone had retired for the night, I was about to open the door when I stopped myself. *Should I bring a candle?* I wondered.

It was hard to decide.

The house would be excessively dark, I guessed, but the candle might be more risk than it was worth. What if someone noticed its flickering light from beneath a closed door? I glanced through the window at the night sky, where a large full moon gleamed. I had to trust that it would provide enough light for me to find the kitchen, where Camille and I had arranged to meet. Without further delay, I stepped into the hall.

In the silence and the shadows, Rousseau Manor seemed even more imposing than by daylight. One misstep, I feared, and I would wake the whole household! *I wish I'd asked Camille to meet me at my room,* I fretted. I felt like an intruder as I crept through the great hall, clinging to the wall so that the moonlight streaming through the tall windows wouldn't cast my shadow. But Camille's directions for reaching the kitchen were perfect, and I soon found myself at its entrance.

"Hello?" I called as I stepped into the cavernous kitchen.

I stood perfectly still, listening in the darkness. Then I heard something.

*"Shhhh."*

"I can't see anything," I whispered as loud as I dared.

A few moments passed; then I felt a hand on my arm. It was Camille! "This way," she replied as she led me through the pitch-black kitchen.

At the top of the basement stairs, Camille lit a candle; it cast precious little light as we started our descent, but it was enough for me to make out each wooden step.

Camille led me past the laundry and the larder to the far side of the basement. "This is where the storage area is," she said, still whispering, even though I was certain no one could hear us all the way down here. "These boxes held Claudia's belongings."

It took no time at all to check each box, because they were all empty. Whoever had taken the diary must've decided against returning it to the basement. Camille looked far more discouraged than I felt.

"What if the diary's gone for good?" she asked.

"Don't think that way—not yet," I replied. "Our search has scarcely begun!"

"But the diary could be *anywhere*," Camille pointed out.

I tapped my chin, lost in thought. "If we don't know *who* took it, then the next best thing is to figure out where it might be hidden," I said slowly. "Whoever heard us reading the diary knew that it was important. That's why they were so quick to take it. So . . . I think they'd want to keep it safe. They wouldn't want to return it to the basement, where anyone could stumble upon it again."

"Then we must ask ourselves, where is the safest place in Rousseau Manor?" Camille mused.

"You'd know that better than I would."

"Madame Colette's dressing parlor or Monsieur

Henri's study," Camille said confidently after a few moments of thought.

We stared at each other for a long moment, until I finally said what we were both thinking. "Then that's where we shall continue our search."

After breakfast the next morning, Camille was waiting for me in the hallway. She grabbed my arm and pulled me into a small alcove.

"It's perfect," she said in a hushed voice. "Madame Colette will be attending a luncheon for the floral appreciation society in town today. By the time she leaves, the housemaids will be finished tidying her dressing parlor. We should have at least an hour undisturbed!"

"What about Monsieur Henri?" I asked.

"Oh, he never goes to her dressing parlor," Camille assured me. "Besides, he'll be occupied at the stables for most of the day, inspecting the new horses."

I smiled at her in admiration. "How *do* you know so much about everything going on in Rousseau Manor?" I asked.

"I just listen," she replied. "You'd be surprised how

much the servants have to know in order to do their jobs."

"I hadn't thought about it like that before," I said. "When Cousin Colette leaves for her luncheon, will you come find me? Then we can go to her room together. Or perhaps I could find a reason to spend the morning with—"

"Claire," someone said.

It was Cousin Colette!

I turned around in shock.

"Would you come with me, please?" she said in an even voice that gave no hint about her feelings. It was impossible to tell how much she had heard.

As Cousin Colette and I walked to her room, my face grew uncomfortably hot just thinking about the plan that Camille and I had devised. Cousin Colette must have noticed, because she looked at me with concern as she placed a hand on my forehead.

"Are you unwell, my dear?" she asked.

"No. I feel fine," I said, ignoring the way my heart was pounding. "It's just—excitement, I suppose. So much has happened! Sometimes when I think about it, I find myself in a state of disbelief."

Cousin Colette nodded understandingly. "That's only to be expected after what you've been through."

I smiled and waited for her to continue, but she just stood there looking at me in the strangest way, as if my very presence in her dressing parlor was a puzzle that she couldn't comprehend.

"Did you . . . want to see me?" I finally asked.

Cousin Colette jolted. "Forgive me, Claire; I have found of late that my thoughts often run away with me, and I am prone to distraction," she said. "I wanted to ask how you are adjusting to life here at Rousseau Manor. Is there anything you need? Anything we can do to make you feel at home?"

"No, not at all!" I assured her. "I know I've just arrived, but I feel quite comfortable here. This is such a beautiful home, and I do love to explore the gardens. And everyone has been so kind to me. You and Cousin Henri most of all, but also the servants, especially Camille . . ."

Too late, I remembered my pledge not to mention Camille to my cousins. My voice trailed off unexpectedly at the look of concern that flickered through Cousin Colette's eyes. But perhaps I'd imagined it, because in half a heartbeat, it was gone.

"I am glad to hear it," she said stiffly. "I would expect nothing less from our staff. Beginning next week, your schedule will start to fill. Your lessons shall begin, and I think I'll have my dressmaker fit you for some new gowns for the summer season. In fact, perhaps . . . perhaps you might like to accompany me to the floral society luncheon today?"

I didn't know what to say.

Under ordinary circumstances, of course I'd love to join Cousin Colette, and I knew that it was deeply kind of her to invite me along.

But the current circumstances were anything but ordinary. I'd made arrangements with Camille, and I was loath to break them.

Cousin Colette must've sensed my hesitation, because she quickly added, "But only if you feel comfortable appearing in society so soon after the loss of your parents. It wouldn't be unheard of, but I know you've been through a great deal."

"Thank you, Cousin, you are very kind," I said. "If you don't mind very much, I think I'd prefer to stay here."

"Of course!" Cousin Colette replied quickly. "It was an insensitive suggestion; forgive me. You *are* still in mourning, I know. But do tell me, is there anything from life at the American Rousseau Manor that you should like to do here?"

I thought for a moment, my fingers fluttering to touch my black armband as they always did when Mother and Father were on my mind. How could I tell Cousin Colette about the way Mother let me help her get ready for her evenings out, even asking my opinion on which jewelry best suited her gown? Or the way Father taught me new French vocabulary every week, incorporating the words into such silly stories that I'd double over from laughter—and never forget them?

To ask this of Cousin Colette and Cousin Henri would be more than an inconvenience.

It would be an imposition.

"Everything here is just as it should be, thank you," I replied. "I can think of nothing else that I need."

A smile lit Cousin Colette's face. "I am very pleased," she told me. "And if there is anything else we can do, you need only say the word."

She turned around to rummage in one of her drawers, retrieving a pair of silk gloves.

"You're leaving already?" I blurted out. I'd thought that Camille had said Cousin Colette would be attending a luncheon, but we'd just finished breakfast.

Cousin Colette tilted her head and looked at me in a funny way. "Yes. We'll be touring some of Paris's finest gardens to view the spring blossoms," she told me. "Unless . . . you'd like me to stay here with you?"

"I'll be fine," I told her. "Enjoy the gardens! I'm sure none of them will compare to the gardens at Rousseau Manor, though. I'm very fond of them already."

"In that case, you and I shall have a picnic in the garden someday soon," Cousin Colette declared. "I'll have Bernadette make all the arrangements."

I followed Cousin Colette into the hallway, then pretended to keep walking in the direction of my room. As soon as she had descended the stairs, I hurried back down the hall to the front window, where I watched the footman help her into the carriage. The *clop-clop-clop* of the horses' hooves echoed back to me as they departed.

*She's gone,* I thought, whirling around to return

to her dressing parlor. A guilty conscience prickled at me—some part of me knew, of course, that it was wrong to sneak into Cousin Colette's dressing parlor when she was away, but I couldn't stop myself. Not when I knew that Cousin Claudia's diary, filled with such enticing secrets, might be hidden there.

And apparently Camille—good, kind Camille, who was more cautious and careful than I'd ever been in my life—must've felt the same way, because she was approaching the door as well, carrying a basket of cleaning supplies.

"There was a—," I began, but Camille put her finger to her lips, so I didn't say another word until we were safe inside Cousin Colette's dressing parlor, with the door closed behind us.

"—tour of the gardens," I continued in a whisper. "That's why she left early."

Camille nodded, her cheeks unusually flushed. "I told Josephine that I'd tidy in here in her place so that we could start searching right away. And I took the liberty of searching Monsieur Henri's study while you were occupied. I hope you're not upset."

"Not at all!" I assured her. "What did you find?"

"Nothing, I'm afraid," she replied. "All his papers are so organized that it made short work of my search."

I glanced around at Cousin Colette's dressing parlor. There were so many drawers and cupboards, jewel cases and hatboxes. The hiding places were endless. I wasn't sure where to begin, so I tried to help Camille, who was dusting Cousin Colette's vanity. But she quickly shooed me away.

"We don't have that much time," she said. "I'll clean. You search."

I worked quickly and quietly, taking extra care to replace everything exactly as I'd found it. Cousin Colette had many fine things, and I marveled at the sight of them. Her hats, trimmed with tulle and lace and silk flowers and colorful plumage from exotic birds, captivated me the most; I found that looking into each hatbox for the lost diary was a bit like opening a birthday present!

Finally, though, I reached the last box on the shelf. I shook it a little before I opened it, hoping to hear the telltale thud of the diary shifting around.

But all I heard was silence.

I opened the box anyway, but it wasn't a hat I found inside.

It was a stack of papers.

I unfolded one with trembling hands. It began: "Dear Mama—"

"Camille!" I cried as loud as I dared. "Come here!"

Camille was by my side in an instant. Together, we began to read.

9 *September* 1898

*Dear Mama,*

*I implore you to reconsider the decision that you and Father have made regarding the fate of my child. I can see no way to part with her (I am certain I will have a daughter), despite your arguments. She is* <u>*my*</u> *child—mine—and she must stay with me here at Rousseau Manor. It is her birthright and her destiny. How could I ever turn my baby over to strangers? For strangers are all* that Nicolas Rousseau and his American wife are to me. I am sure you are right that my father's cousins are fine people, but I cannot give them my child. I will not do it.

It is not too late to tell the world the truth: that in one season I was wed and widowed; that my great grief over my husband's death shall be soothed by the greater joy of our child's birth when the December snows come.

Please, Mama, think on this request and come to me with your understanding and compassion. Where my child goes, I will go too—even if I must leave my home once more.

Love,
Claudia

I tried to speak, but the words stuck in my throat. "But Nicolas Rousseau was my father," I managed to squeak out, pointing at the name with trembling fingers.

"So, Madame Claudia's baby came to live with *you*?" she said, gasping.

I shook my head. "I don't think so," I replied. "We would've grown up together—but I was the only child at the Rousseau Manor in America."

Camille's eyes shone happily. "Madame Colette and Monsieur Henri must've changed their minds, then!" she cried. "They relented and allowed Madame Claudia to keep her baby!"

"Did they, though?" I asked slowly. "Or did they find another home for the poor little one?"

"I do hope Madame Claudia was able to keep her baby for as long as she lived," Camille said in concern.

A new idea struck me then, and I sat up straighter. "Do you think Claudia left again?" I asked. "Like she warns in the letter? And took the baby with her?"

"But we know Madame Claudia died," Camille said. "So where is the baby now?"

It was a mystery that we just couldn't solve with the little information we had.

"Someone knows," I finally said. "Someone,

somewhere, knows what happened to Claudia's baby. In fact, I can think of at least two people."

"Monsieur Henri and Madame Colette," Camille whispered.

"We have no choice but to ask them," I said. It was as simple as that.

But Camille did not agree. "No," she said, more firmly than I'd ever heard her say anything. "We mustn't."

"But why not?"

"I won't speak of it!" Camille said, and then she clamped her lips shut.

Her short words felt like a slap. "Oh," was all I could say. Then I folded the letter and returned it to the box. I didn't want Camille to see that my feelings were hurt, but I was hopeless to hide it.

"Claire . . ."

"We should go," I said, glancing at the porcelain clock.

In the hallway, Camille tried again. "Don't be upset," she said. "I didn't mean to say it like that. I just—I wish I didn't have to tell you this, but I don't think I have a choice."

"You don't have to tell me if you don't want to."

"I think you need to know."

We stopped walking. Camille glanced around to make sure no one was nearby before she continued speaking.

"That day when you went into Madame Claudia's room for the first time," she began, "I didn't tell you everything. The truth is . . . The truth is that I was the one who put Claudia's old things in her room. I thought it would be the perfect room for you. I didn't know about Claudia then, and when I showed the Rousseaus what I'd done, they took it very poorly."

"What do you mean, 'poorly'?"

Camille closed her eyes, as if the memory were too painful to bear. "Madame Colette wept and Monsieur Henri flew into a rage. The shock was so great, yet not as great as their grief for Madame Claudia. That is why no one speaks of her, you see."

"And I suppose that's why no one is permitted to enter Cousin Claudia's old room," I said thoughtfully. I could see now why Camille was so cautious of doing anything that might upset Cousin Colette and Cousin

Henri. *How peculiar,* I thought. All I wanted was to remember Mother and Father and all the love that we'd shared, and yet it seemed that my cousins wanted only to forget.

But I couldn't forget Cousin Claudia. Not after seeing her things and her pretty room; not after feeling such a strong and strange connection to it—a connection that I still couldn't understand.

And not after reading her diary and her letter. Not after learning that her child was supposed to grow up alongside me, like the sister I'd always wanted.

*What has become of that little baby?* I wondered, and I was about to ask Camille what she thought we should do next when, suddenly, I heard it. It was faint but unmistakable: the delicate sound of Father's violin.

And it was coming from the direction of my room.

I broke away from Camille and ran, ran as fast I could. If there was any chance, any chance at all—

I threw open the door so fast that it banged against the wall.

Only to discover that my room was empty; the violin safely tucked in its case, just the way I'd left it.

I was more disappointed than I cared to admit. I squeezed my eyes shut tight so that the tears welling there wouldn't have a chance to fall. Camille had followed me, but I didn't realize it until I felt her hand on my shoulder.

"I heard it too," she said.

6

"Are you all right?" Camille continued quietly.

"Of course. I'm fine," I replied in a rush, but the truth was that I felt unbearably foolish, standing in my bright and cheerful room with the sunlight streaming through the windows. What was happening to me that I could entertain such a silly thought? There were no such things as ghosts. Even as my cheeks reddened, a smile flickered across my face as I thought about how Father would've chuckled to hear this story. His laugh was so deep and rich that he never laughed alone. Just thinking about him made me feel a bit less foolish.

"I think I'd like to take a walk outside," I said as I fanned my blushing face. "Would you care to join me?"

"I wish I could, but I need to help Mama in the kitchen," Camille said wistfully. "She's planned an especially elaborate dessert for tonight—though why she wants me there to get in the way, I don't know."

"Don't say such things," I chided her in a friendly way. "I'm sure your mother is glad to have your help. I know I always am!"

"If we finish early, I'll look for you in the gardens," Camille promised.

"Camille?" I asked hesitantly as she moved toward the door. "We didn't imagine hearing that music, right? Do you know where it could have been coming from?"

Camille paused and stared into the distance, deep in thought. At last she spoke. "I'm not sure. There's a phonograph in Monsieur Henri's study, but I wouldn't think that we could hear it all the way up here. Besides, he should still be in the stables."

"Maybe one of the housemaids was cleaning it and . . . and it started to play on its own," I said, grasping for a theory that might make sense.

"Maybe," Camille replied, but she didn't sound convinced.

We walked into the hallway together, but soon after we descended the stairs, Camille and I parted ways. She went in the direction of the kitchen, while I pushed through the double doors and stepped into the warm spring sunshine. I took a deep breath and exhaled slowly as I walked, trying to quiet my mind. My thoughts were such a muddle, as if tossed about on a stormy sea.

From the haunting music wafting through the halls—

To the letter filled with Cousin Claudia's heartfelt pleas—

To the unknown fate of her little baby—

And, of course, the missing diary—

How would I ever sort it all out?

For reasons I didn't understand, I simply had to find the answers. *It will do me good to sit a spell in the flower garden,* I thought, *surrounded by the blossoms that Mother loved best. She always did know how to help me calm my mind.*

But as I approached the tranquil gardens, a harsh voice shattered my reverie.

"That's not good enough. I want to know exactly *where* you were."

I ducked behind a tall hedge and held myself still as a statue, listening to every word. The voice that answered was mumbled and hard to hear until—

"Speak up, son!"

"I—just—it—"

"A simple question deserves a simple answer, Alexandre."

*The groundskeeper's son!* I thought, remembering how Camille and I had seen him in the hallway outside my room yesterday. But I pushed the memory out of my mind so that I could focus on what his father, Phillipe, was saying.

"Just a few weeks we've been here, and already you see fit to shirk your duties! Do you think the Rousseaus will look kindly on that? Do you think they will allow us to stay if—"

"Father, I'm sorry," came Alexandre's reply. He sounded miserable. "I—here, give me your trowel. I'll finish the weeding myself, no matter how long it takes—"

"Alexandre! Your fingers!"

*What's wrong with his fingers?* I wondered curiously, wishing that I could see through the dense hedge.

"It's nothing, Father."

"But why are they so red? Have you been in the stinging nettles? I don't see any welts—and only the left hand is afflicted. . . ."

71

Suddenly, it all made sense. Papa's fingers—the fingers on his left hand—always turned red and tender whenever he played his violin after a long absence. Now I knew where the music had come from and even why we'd seen Alexandre in the east wing.

"Come. We'll go to the kitchen and ask your mother for a poultice," Philippe said. "Not a word to her of your dillydallying; it would break her heart to hear that her son was acting like a layabout—"

But Alexandre didn't need a poultice, not if his fingers were red from playing my father's violin. And I didn't want to waste this opportunity to ask him my questions.

"Excuse me," I said brazenly as I stepped around the hedge, startling both Philippe and Alexandre. "I am sorry, Philippe. I owe you an apology."

*"Me?"* Philippe echoed in disbelief. He immediately removed his cap and clutched it in his hands. "Mademoiselle Claire, you are mistaken, I am sure—"

I shook my head vehemently. "Not at all; you see, it was I who called Alexandre away from his work."

Alexandre looked at me in astonishment, and for just an instant I was ashamed to be caught in such a bold-faced lie. But surely he would appreciate my efforts if it spared him a punishment.

"He has been most kind, introducing me to the native plants of France and teaching me their names, at my request, of course," I continued. "This is my home-land now, and I want to know everything about it."

Philippe looked from me to Alexandre and back to me again.

"But I see now that my desire to learn about French plants has interrupted Alexandre's duties, and for that I apologize," I said. "It won't happen again."

Philippe cleared his throat. "Not at all, Mademoiselle Claire," he said in a much calmer, kinder voice. "It will be Alexandre's pleasure to teach you about plants whenever you desire."

"Wonderful!" I said brightly. "Might we continue now? There's a flower that I've been so very curious about."

"Of course," Philippe replied with a slight bow. Then he turned to his son. "I'll be in the topiary garden when you are free."

"Yes, Father," Alexandre replied, speaking for the first time since my interruption.

We stood together in silence while Philippe left. The moment he was out of view, I spun around to face Alexandre.

"Have you been playing my violin?"

"Just—once! Twice. I swear it was only twice! I played so softly, I hoped no one would hear me," he explained in a panic. "Forgive me, mademoiselle. It will never happen again!"

"There's no need to ask for forgiveness," I said right away, surprised at his outburst. "But why is it a secret? You play very well—as well as my—"

But I couldn't finish the sentence.

There was a long, uncomfortable silence until Alexandre finally spoke. "My father does not approve," he said, staring at the ground. "In our old home there was a musician who lived in the apartment above ours. He used to give me lessons on the violin, and all I had to do in return was feed his cat on the nights when he played with the symphony."

I waited quietly for Alexandre to continue.

"I loved it, more than anything," he said at last. "But Papa said it was a waste of time. We'd never be able to afford a violin, or even proper lessons on a regular schedule. Then the Great Flood came. . . . We lost our home, and so did my music teacher. Papa said I should count it as a blessing—that it was time to put away such foolish pastimes."

"That's nonsense," I said hotly, but caught myself quickly. "You seem to me to be quite talented."

For the first time, something close to a smile crossed Alexandre's face, but he quickly shook his head. "I haven't played in months, Mademoiselle Claire," he said. "But when I heard you playing in the garden the other day—"

"That was you!" I exclaimed, forgetting my manners as I interrupted him. "I *thought* there was someone near."

"I was on my way to water the roses when I heard your violin," he said. "Just a few notes made my fingers start to tremble. I longed to play again, and I couldn't get the thought out of my mind."

"So that's why you snuck into my room when I was not there," I realized.

He nodded, but he refused to meet my eye. And was that sunburn that made his cheeks look so pink, or was he blushing from embarrassment? "It was wrong of me, I know. I should've asked your permission, at the very least. It will never happen again."

"That's what would truly be wrong," I replied. "You are always welcome to play Father's violin. In fact, now that I know you enjoy playing so much, I will leave it near the door of my room so that you can play whenever you want." It would be the perfect solution!

"Thank you, Mademoiselle Claire, but such a thing would be impossible," he said. "Father watches me all the time, and I fear that he will keep an even closer eye on me now."

I pursed my lips, unhappy to see Alexandre so resigned to a life without music. For Father, there was nothing in the world like playing his violin—nothing at all. It brought him such joy, and not only that, it brought joy to all who heard him. If Alexandre felt the same way—and it certainly seemed that he did—it would be a crime to keep him from it.

Right then and there, I made a silent vow. *I will find a way for you to play, Alexandre,* I promised. *No matter what!*

But all I said to Alexandre was, "We shall see about that."

Then I began walking toward the flower garden. "I was telling your father the truth, you know. I have been quite curious about some of the plants here, particularly a flower that was very dear to my mother. Do you think you might help me identify it?"

"Why, certainly," Alexandre replied as he fell into step beside me. "If I can, of course. I began apprenticing with my father only when we came here, so I'm really just learning all about plants myself."

We walked beneath the bower, and I led him right over to the sweetly scented blooms. "This one here," I said. "Do you know what kind of flower this is?"

Alexandre shook his head. "'Fraid not," he replied. Then he reached into his pocket and pulled out a slim volume, yellowed with age. "But this might help."

"What is it?" I asked curiously.

"It's the last groundkeeper's journal," Alexandre explained as he began to flip through the dirt-stained pages. "Mostly, he wrote about how to care for the topiary garden. But I've found other notes in it too, and even some drawings."

We sat together for quite some time as we looked through the journal. I didn't see any sketches of

Mother's favorite flowers, but the groundskeeper's notes were very charming to read.

*A favorite of Little C,* he wrote next to a sketch of poppies.

*Little C has asked for a peacock in the topiary. What will she think of next!*

"Who's this 'Little C?' I wonder," I said.

"Camille, I'm sure," Alexandre replied offhandedly. "This was her father's journal."

My mouth dropped open in surprise. "Her father?" I repeated. "Her *father* was the groundskeeper here?"

Alexandre nodded. "For many years, I'm told, until he died of influenza. Father and I found his journal after we took over the groundskeeper's duties."

"Might I borrow it?" I asked impulsively. "I think Camille should have the chance to read it."

"Of course," Alexandre replied. "But I'll need it back before too long. We'll be starting the elephant next."

"I shouldn't need to keep it for more than a day or two," I told him. It was a very slim volume, after all.

And the last thing I wanted was for Alexandre to get in more trouble.

7

I bade farewell to Alexandre and went back to Rousseau Manor so that I could show Camille her father's journal. I knew she would be delighted to read all the little notes he'd written about her! First, though, I decided to stop by my room so that I could leave my parasol and gloves there. As I passed by Cousin Henri's study, I heard three voices talking over one another with such agitation that they carried all the way through the closed door. I simply had to pause and listen.

"We have no choice but to tell them—"

"I *told* you this would happen—"

"The question is, how much do they already know?"

Two of the voices were familiar to me—Cousin Henri's and Cousin Colette's, of course.

But who was the third?

"We cannot assume that—"

"Would you *please* be so kind as to lower your voice!"

*Drat,* I thought—though I couldn't help smiling; Cousin Henri's words had carried through the door even as he implored the others to be quiet. Sure enough, after that all I could hear were muffled whispers.

*Who* are *they talking to?* I wondered. And perhaps even more pressing: *How can I find out?*

I scanned the long hallway as I tried to figure out what to do next. It would never do to stand right outside Cousin Henri's study as though I was eavesdropping, and I didn't dare interrupt such a serious and urgent conversation.

Then I spotted it: a large potted plant near the end of the hall. If I could hide behind it and *if* the people in the room went the other way down the hall when they came out, I would be able to see who else was in the study with my cousins. Just as I tucked myself behind the waxy leaves, I heard the door open. I held my breath, pressed myself even flatter against the wall, and peeked through the leaves.

Cousin Henri entered the hall first, holding the door open for Cousin Colette. She stepped out of the study and paused to say something to the person behind her. My impatience was an agony as I waited—waited—waited—

Then the third person stepped out of the room, and even through the leaves I could see her clearly. She looked familiar—I'd met her when I first arrived at Rousseau Manor—but for the life of me, I couldn't recall her name.

Suddenly, Cousin Colette reached out and took hold of the woman's hand. "Thank you, Marie," she said fervently. "The decisions ahead will not be easy ones, but we are so grateful for the warning you've given us."

Marie! Of course! The pastry chef—and Camille's mother!

"Of course, madame," Marie said, but there was a stiffness to her shoulders, as if she was trying to control her emotions. "Please let me know what you decide."

Then Marie disappeared down the hall—in the opposite direction from me, fortunately—while Cousin Colette and Cousin Henri retreated back into the study, closing the door firmly behind them.

I breathed a sigh of relief that no one had seen me,

but my relief was all too quickly replaced by intense curiosity. What did Cousin Colette mean? What difficult decisions were ahead? And what had Marie warned them about?

All I knew for certain was that I had to talk to Camille at once. I *had* to tell her everything! Another mystery at Rousseau Manor, and this time Camille's own mother was involved. Perhaps Camille already knew what they were talking about, and if not, I couldn't think of anyone else I'd rather solve it with.

I set off for the kitchen, reminding myself to act normally if I should see Marie there. Luckily, Marie was occupied at the stove, and Camille was in the process of bringing Baby Sophie back to her mother; I was able to catch Camille's eye and gesture for her to join me in the hall without attracting anyone else's attention.

"I'm sorry I couldn't join you in the garden!" she said right away. "As soon as I finished helping Mama, it was time to look after Sophie. I would've brought her in the pram, but the wheel needs fixing."

I shook my head. "Never mind that," I replied. "You

won't believe what just happened." And then I proceeded to tell Camille everything I'd heard. She stared at me in disbelief.

"I haven't the faintest idea what they were talking about," Camille said. "But I'll keep my ears open, and if I find out—"

"Couldn't you just ask your mother?" I asked, letting my impatience get the better of me.

"How?" Camille pointed out rationally. "Mama would want to know how I found out about their conversation."

I grinned sheepishly. "Yes, you're right. It would never do to tell them that I was listening at the door," I admitted. Then I sighed. So many unsolved mysteries, so many unanswered questions. It seemed to me that one forthright conversation would do wonders to clarify everything!

"Don't worry, though," Camille assured me. "Mama always says that the truth will come out, and she's never been wrong yet."

A door down the hall opened then, and Bernadette entered the hallway. She started at the sight of me. "Mademoiselle Claire! What are you doing down here?" she exclaimed. Her voice was so loud that everyone in the kitchen looked over at us. "Have you come for something to eat?"

"Eat?" I repeated.

"You missed lunch," she said pointedly. Bernadette would never dare to reprimand me, of course, but I could tell she was displeased.

"Missed lunch!" Marie cried from the stove. "No, that will never do. Mrs. Plourde—"

"Yes, of course," the cook replied as she started fixing a tray.

All this fuss for me! I felt terrible. "I'm so sorry," I told them. "Please don't go to any trouble."

"It's no trouble at all, but you should have a little something to eat now," Bernadette said. "Not too much, though. It won't be long until dinner is served. In fact, I was just on my way to help you dress for dinner."

"Goodness, I didn't realize it was so late already," I replied. "Thank you, Bernadette."

Bernadette nodded and then glanced at Camille. "You worked very hard today," she said. "I know your mother was grateful for your help."

"Thank you," Camille said, ducking her head. "I tried my best."

Bernadette and I took our leave then, and she accompanied me back to my room. It wasn't until we arrived that I realized I was still holding the gardening journal under my arm. In all the excitement, I'd completely forgotten to show it to Camille. *I suppose it can wait until later,* I thought with disappointment as I put the book on my bedside table. All the while, as Bernadette helped me dress and fixed my hair, I couldn't stop thinking about what Camille had said: *The truth will come out.*

But how? And when?

An hour later, I joined my cousins in the dining room for dinner. I was still deeply distracted by my curiosity about what I'd heard earlier, yet Cousin Henri and Cousin Colette were perfectly composed, as though nothing unusual had happened.

"And so I think perhaps next year we will tour the gardens a week or two later," Cousin Colette was saying. "The unexpected freeze last month meant that some of my favorite flowers were not yet in bloom."

"Pity," remarked Cousin Henri.

I tried my hardest not to fidget. Under the table, where no one could see, I knotted my napkin in my hands, but it did little to relieve my agitation.

Then they both turned to me.

"And how did you spend your day, Claire?" asked Cousin Colette.

I swallowed hard. And then I began to speak. The words that tumbled out of my mouth shocked even me.

"What happened to Claudia's baby?" I blurted out.

There was a tinkling of silver on china as Cousin Colette dropped her fork, but after that the room was silent. Perfectly, utterly, and horribly silent. My cousins stared at me.

"I want to know," I pressed on. "I *need* to know. The baby was meant to live with me—in my father's safekeeping—and yet, as far as I know, it never came to pass. Where is the baby?"

"Excuse us, please," Cousin Henri spoke at last, but his words weren't directed at me. Instead, he was addressing the footmen, who wasted no time leaving the dining room.

Tiny beads of sweat dotted Cousin Henri's forehead; he wiped them with his handkerchief before he turned back to me. "Claire—," he began, then stopped. He tried again. "Claire." But he seemed unable to say more than my name.

"How do you know all this?" Cousin Colette asked. She was clutching the tabletop for support, and her eyes seemed especially shiny in the candlelight, but her voice was calm and steady. Strong.

I braced myself. This was the problem with rushing off and doing something without thinking it all the way through. *How many times did Mother warn you about this?* I chided myself. But it was too late now; I couldn't take back what I'd said. And if I was hoping for honesty from my cousins, it was the least I could offer them in return.

"I found Cousin Claudia's diary, and I read part of it," I said, keeping Camille out of it. "But it disappeared from Claudia's room before I could read the rest, so I've been searching for it."

I paused to take a breath. This next part would be even harder to say, but I had no choice. "I looked in your dressing parlor, Cousin Colette, and I found

Claudia's letter to you. The one where she begged to keep her child here at Rousseau Manor."

Cousin Colette pressed her hand over her eyes before I could see her reaction to my words.

Such a long silence followed that my curiosity melted away, replaced by something altogether more troubling: anxiety. The questions racing through my mind were suddenly very different: What if my cousins were too angry to let me stay? What if they sent me away? Where would I go if I wore out my welcome here?

Why did I *always* have to rush forward without thinking through all the consequences?

At last Cousin Colette lowered her hand. She and Cousin Henri exchanged a long glance, full of meaning that I couldn't understand. But they could, and that was the important part, I suppose, because Henri finally began to speak.

"I am sure that my cousins Nicolas and Annabelle raised you better than this, dear Claire," Cousin Henri said. His reproach wasn't born of anger, but disappointment, and suddenly I was filled with tremendous shame. Cousin Henri was right; I never would've dreamed of snooping in Mother's dressing parlor like that, and it was horrible that I'd done such a thing to Cousin Colette.

"I'm sorry," I whispered.

"This is your home, and you should feel comfortable and at ease here," Cousin Henri continued. "However, we do expect you to respect our privacy as well."

"It won't happen again," I promised them both.

Cousin Colette rose abruptly. I followed her with my eyes as she circled the table and, pulling out the chair to my right, sat beside me. Cousin Henri moved his place, too, so that he was directly on my other side. My heart started beating harder, faster. Something was about to happen. Something of the utmost importance.

And I could scarcely wait to find out what.

"But your questions and curiosity are understandable, my dear girl," Cousin Colette said as she reached for my hand. "And we will do our best to answer them. In truth, we've been carrying this secret for far too long, and I, for one, shall be glad to be free of it."

Cousin Henri nodded his agreement.

"Claudia's baby did go to America with Nicolas Rousseau," Cousin Colette said. Her green eyes never wavered, never left my face. "It was you."

I blinked in astonishment. *Surely* I had misheard—
*Surely* I was mistaken—

"It was you," Cousin Colette repeated, and the first tear escaped from her eyes, trailing down her powdered cheek in a silvery streak. Her grip on my hand tightened. "It was you."

*I* was Claudia's longed-for daughter?

*Claudia* was my *mother*?

My whole world changed forever in that instant. I pressed my fingers to my temples as I tried to understand. If Claudia was my mother . . . then Cousin Henri and Cousin Colette were my grandparents. Not my cousins at all! No wonder, then, that they had so readily agreed to be my guardians when Mother and Father died, despite all our friends and business connections in America. And Mother and Father—I had not been born to them. They were my grandfather's cousins.

I shook my head. I was still a Rousseau; this shocking revelation didn't change that. In fact, I was a Rousseau who had been born in this very house, to a mother who had wanted me very much.

When I finally spoke, I nearly choked on the words. "You sent me away from her? All she wanted was to keep her baby, and you sent me *away*? From my *mother*?"

The tears were streaming freely down Cousin Colette's face now, but she made no effort to wipe them away. "Do not think it was an easy thing to do," she told me. "Do not think that I haven't wondered, every day of my life, if we made the right choice."

Still, though, I couldn't understand how this had come to pass. "Claudia wrote that she would take me away if you tried, but—"

"But she died," Cousin Henri interrupted me. "Claudia died giving birth, and all her dreams with her. Including mothering you, which she wanted to do more than anything."

"She would've been a wonderful mother," Cousin Colette said. "And I doubt that, in the face of her motherly love and devotion, we would've been able to follow through with our original plan."

"But she died," Cousin Henri repeated. "And you were very much alive and in need of a family. Colette and I—how could we care for you properly when our hearts were broken beyond repair? How could we raise you in a house that had descended into the depths of grief?"

Cousin Colette spoke up. "Then there were Nicolas and Annabelle to consider. They longed to be parents but had not been blessed with children. If we turned you over to their loving care, we could make their dreams come true. We could give you a chance at a childhood that was not shadowed by grief. I will show you, Claire, the letter they wrote after I asked if they would raise you as their own. I have kept it all these years because the sheer joy they experienced at the mere *thought* of you coming into their lives—"

She paused to wipe my tears with her hand-kerchief, and that's when I realized that I was crying, too.

"They loved you very much, you know," Cousin Henri said. "You were everything to them."

"How do you know that?" I dared to ask.

Cousin Colette rested her hand on my cheek. "Because they wrote to us every month to keep us informed of your progress," she told me. "So you see, though you don't know us very well at all, we have been following your life for years. It was the next best thing to having you here. And when I would doubt our decision, all I had to do was read one of Annabelle's letters to be assured that you were leading a very happy life indeed. It *was* a happy life, wasn't it?"

I thought of Mother and Father and the richness of our life together: grand adventures in the city and cozy nights at home. Holidays and celebrations and, most of all, the ordinary days, when Father's music would drift through the garden as I helped Mother tend her flowers. "Yes," I said, smiling through my tears. "Yes, it was."

"And it will be again," Cousin Colette promised me. "Henri and I shall see to that."

Something wonderful and surprising happened then: All the stiffness and distance between us seemed to melt away in an instant. Without that long-kept secret standing between us, there would be a chance now for us to become family . . . the way we were always meant to be.

I looked up. "May I call you Grandmother?" I asked hesitantly. "And Grandfather?"

They exchanged another glance, but it was easy,

this time, to know what it meant.

"Nothing would please us more," my grandmother said.

Grandfather Henri rose from his chair. "Are you hungry, my dear?" he asked kindly. "Thirsty? I'll send for the footmen—"

"I don't think I could eat a single bite," I said.

"That's perfectly understandable; you've had quite a shock," Grandmother Colette said. "I'll have Bernadette bring a tray to your room later, in case you recover your appetite."

"Thank you," I said. I climbed the stairs two at a time, but I didn't go to my room. Instead, I went directly to Camille's room. The only thought in my mind was telling Camille this tremendous news at once!

I rapped on the door and waited impatiently for an answer. It was Marie who opened it a few moments later. She took one look at me and motioned for me to come in.

"Mademoiselle Claire!" she exclaimed. "What's the matter? Is everything all right?"

"It's—" I paused and placed my hand over my chest, where my heart was thundering wildly—partly from running up the stairs and partly from the shock I'd had.

"Come. Sit," Marie said, wrapping her arm around my shoulders as she led me over to a comfortable settee. I caught a glimpse of my reflection in a gilt-framed mirror. My eyes were watery; my cheeks were flushed; even my hair was disheveled. No wonder Marie was so concerned; I truly looked a fright!

Just then Camille came into the room. "Claire!" she said, clearly surprised to see me.

I jumped up from the settee at the sound of her voice. "Camille!" I cried. "It's me! *I'm* Claudia's baby!"

A stunned silence descended over Camille and her mother. I pressed ahead, the words tumbling out of my mouth almost faster than I could think them.

"I asked my cous—I mean, they're my grandparents now, you see. I asked Grandfather Henri and Grandmother Colette about Claudia's baby, and they told me everything! *I'm* the baby she wanted to keep, but she died and they were so sad that they sent me to live with the American Rousseaus, who had no children of their own!"

"Oh, Claire!" Camille exclaimed as she rushed

forward to hug me. "I can hardly believe—"

"Neither can I!" I interrupted her. "To think, I've been so consumed by this mystery, not ever dreaming that I was a part of it."

"It's almost as if you *knew* in some way," she said.

I shook my head. "I wish that were true, but I had no idea," I told her. "None at all. I keep wanting to pinch myself. None of this seems real."

"And yet it must be," Camille said.

"Everything is changed now," I continued. "I mean—Mother and Father—I'll always, always love them. They will *always* be my parents."

"Of course! Nothing can change that," Camille assured me.

"But I had another set of parents too. Another mother. Claudia. I wish I could've known her. I'd give anything to . . ." I trailed off.

"Did Madame Colette tell you if she has the diary?" Camille asked suddenly.

"No. She didn't mention it. Why?"

"Because you simply must read it now," Camille said. "It's more important than ever. Think of it! Madame Claudia's own words! Remember what she wrote? About how excited she was to meet you?"

"Yes," I whispered as a lump formed in my throat. I blinked back fresh tears. "I do."

"There's still a chance to get to know your mother, Claire, at least a little," Camille told me. "And all you have to do is find her diary."

"Please excuse me," Marie said abruptly as she rose from the settee. Only then did I realize how quiet she had been since my big announcement. Without another word, she rushed across the room.

"Mama?" Camille asked, her voice full of concern.

But Marie was already gone.

8

$\mathcal{T}$he next day was such a busy one for Camille that she didn't have a moment to spare for me until after dinner. Marie needed her help at every turn, keeping Camille in the kitchen for the entire day! Every time I snuck downstairs to check if Camille was still busy, I felt a strange sense of longing when I saw the way she and her mother worked together. It made me miss my mothers—both of them—very much.

At last dinner had been served and eaten, and Camille had the evening to herself. She came to find me at once, and we wasted no time in retreating to Claudia's room. It was still light outside, though the sun had begun to set; impulsively, I opened the heavy drapes so that the last golden beams of sunlight could enter Claudia's room.

"Are you sure?" Camille asked. She glanced nervously at the door. "Someone might see—"

"This was my mother's room," I replied. "Until Grandfather Henri or Grandmother Colette tell me I'm not allowed to be here, I have every intention of spending as much time in it as I possibly can."

"Of course. I understand," Camille said quickly. "I *wish* you could get the diary back. It seems so wrong that it was taken from you."

"I wish so too," I said. "But I'm glad to be here, in this room, with all of Claudia's favorite things, at least." I still didn't know what I should call her; it felt wrong to call her Mother when I was still missing my other mother, the woman who had loved and raised me. Grandmother Colette had assured me that in time I would grow used to this new way of looking at the world. But for now it felt very strange and unfamiliar.

I reached for one of the wind-up animals on the bureau, a peacock, and twisted the metal key in its back. It strutted in a circle as the clockwork mechanism inside it spun around. Soon Camille and I were racing to wind up every animal until they were all moving at once. The marching peacock ... the monkey with its cymbals ... the kissing swans ...

"It's getting dark," Camille said. "Would you like me to fetch a lamp?"

"I suppose," I said as I walked over to the window and looked out at the grounds. "Let's enjoy the sunset first, though." Most of the gardens were cloaked in dusky twilight, but the topiary garden sat on a bit of a hill so that the last beams of sunlight still illuminated the animals. The majestic peacock, the silly monkey, the graceful swans—

That's when it hit me, all of a sudden; and I was so shocked that I gasped.

"Camille!" I cried.

She looked up in alarm. "What? What is it?"

"The topiary animals! They're the same as the ones in Claudia's wind-up menagerie!"

In a blink, Camille scooped up all of the toy animals and brought them over to the window. Sure enough, each toy had a matching topiary in the garden outside.

"That is no coincidence!" Camille said excitedly. "I can't believe I didn't notice it before. My papa must've done it on purpose—sculpted all those bushes to match Claudia's favorite toys!"

Camille's father. The groundskeeper. Of course.

The topiary menagerie was all his doing.

And his journal was still in my room!

Somehow, in all of yesterday's excitement, I had completely forgotten to give it to her.

"Camille, wait here. I'll be right back," I promised. Then I ran all the way to my room, where I grabbed Pierre's journal and a lamp that one of the housemaids had already lit. The flame flickered as I hurried back down the hallway, reminding me to walk slowly and carefully. Camille was standing by the door of Claudia's room, waiting expectantly for my return. She closed the door right after me; it was clear that Camille was still worried that we'd get in trouble for being there.

"Oh, good. You brought a lamp," Camille said. "I was just about to get one."

"That's not all I brought," I told her as I held out her father's journal. "Here. This is for you."

"Papa's journal!" Camille cried. "Yes. Alexandre showed it to me before you arrived. He and his father are using it to fix the topiary garden. I didn't get much of a chance to look at it, though."

"You should," I told her. "I asked Alexandre if you could borrow it, and he said yes."

"I'm so grateful to you," she said. "My papa has been gone for a long time now. Reading this will be like having the chance to talk to him again. Come. Let's look at it together."

We sat side by side, just as we had with Claudia's diary. Camille marveled at everything about the journal—the entries written in her father's hand, the smudges of dirt in the shape of his fingerprints, and especially the notes about 'Little C.' But as we read, a new thought occurred to me. *What if 'Little C' wasn't Camille after all?* I thought. *What if 'Little C' was Claudia?* It would make so much sense, especially if the topiary garden had been planted to charm Claudia by matching up to her favorite toys.

I looked at Camille out of the corner of my eye. Should I tell her my suspicion? I had no proof, and I would hate to hurt her feelings when she was so delighted by her father's journal.

As it turned out, there was nothing I needed to say, for Camille glanced up with a thoughtful look on her face. "You know, Claire," she began, as if she were still puzzling out whatever was on her mind, "I think perhaps Little C might have been your mother."

"Oh," I replied. "Yes, I suppose so." I watched Camille carefully to see if this would upset her. But instead of sadness settling over her face, all I saw there was joy.

"Just think of it!" Camille exclaimed. "My own papa, toiling in the garden to make your mother happy when she was a little girl!"

Suddenly, there came a knock at the door. Beside me, Camille froze, and a look of fear careened across her face.

"Don't worry," I whispered. "I'll see to it that you won't get in trouble for being here."

Then I strode across the room and opened the door. Bernadette was waiting on the other side of it.

"Madame Colette thought I might find you two here," she said with a quizzical look on her face. "Please come with me. She has requested an audience with you both."

I turned to Camille, who looked paler than usual. "Come along," I told her. "Everything will be fine."

But behind my brave face, I was starting to worry. My grandparents had never said that *I* couldn't visit Claudia's room, but they hadn't said that I could, either.

And after how upset they'd been with Camille . . .

When we reached Grandmother Colette's dressing parlor, Bernadette excused herself. I squirmed with discomfort at the memory of the last time Camille and I had visited this room: in secret, sneaking about to search for Claudia's diary.

If we'd only known then what we were about to uncover!

*Grandmother Colette will surely scold us,* I thought with dread. Beside me, I was certain that Camille was thinking the same thing. We exchanged a glance and a wobbly smile, and then we stepped into the room together.

Grandmother Colette was sitting at her dressing table when we entered. In the mirror, I could see her reflection as she looked up at us. I braced myself, waiting for the reprimand I expected her to deliver.

But instead of speaking harsh words, Grandmother Colette's lips parted in a smile. "Good evening, girls," she said. "I thought I might brush your hair tonight."

"Together?" Camille cried happily. My confusion must've been all over my face, because she quickly turned to me and explained. "Sometimes when Madame

Colette stays in, she will send for me and brush my hair before bed."

She began to walk toward the bench beside the dressing table, but I hesitated. *This is a special time for Camille and Grandmother Colette,* I thought. *It's not right for me to intrude.*

As Camille sat upon the bench, though, she beckoned for me to join her. Since she didn't seem to see my presence as an intrusion, I crossed the room to sit beside her.

Grandmother Colette unpinned Camille's hair from its plait. Then she began to brush it with long, even strokes. "I see you girls have become fast friends already," she remarked.

Camille and I smiled at each other—as best we could, anyway, since Camille couldn't move her head while Grandmother Colette was brushing her hair.

"Yes," I answered Grandmother Colette. "I wish I'd known that Camille was here when I first set foot on the steamer. It would've made the journey from America so much easier to bear."

"I'm glad of it," continued my grandmother. "I suspected that you might get along. It is not an easy thing to feel alone in the world. It's my hope, now that you know each other, that your hearts will never be burdened by such feelings."

I felt Grandmother Colette's brush against the back of my head then, and I closed my eyes.

"Such short hair!" she exclaimed. "I can't say I've ever brushed hair so short. Perhaps long ago, when Claudia was very small and her hair had just begun to grow. I must say it suits you, Claire, and is very stylish. Camille, have you ever fancied having short hair?"

"No. I can't say that I have," she replied, twirling a strand of her long locks around her finger.

"That's good, then. We can't have you girls looking *too* much alike. I suspect you'll soon be as close as two peas in a pod . . . if you aren't already."

Grandmother Colette continued to brush my hair for a few more minutes. Then she turned away to place the brush on her dressing table. "All done, my dears," she said. "Let's have a look."

Camille and I rose from the bench and stood before her. There was something unusual in Grandmother Colette's eyes, some flicker of emotion that I couldn't quite name.

"Beautiful, beautiful girls, the both of you," she said.

We curtsied together and turned to go, but Grandmother Colette held up her hand. "One moment, please," she said. She opened one of the drawers of her dressing table and pulled out a silver-backed mirror. She cradled it in her palms for a moment, staring at it. Then she held it out to me.

"This belonged to Claudia," she said. "I'd like you to have it."

I took the mirror from her, turning it over in my hands. The back was covered in elaborate engravings of a wreath of forget-me-nots that encircled the letter *C*. The weight of the cool, heavy silver felt good in my hands, comforting almost.

"Claire should have the hairbrush, too," Camille said suddenly. She turned to me. "There's a matching hairbrush. They were part of a set. It's in my room. I'll get it."

"No."

Grandmother Colette cupped Camille's cheeks in her hands and looked deep into her eyes. "I have given that hairbrush to you, Camille, and I insist that you keep it."

Camille looked confused—no, concerned. Then, for the first time ever, I heard her disagree with my grandmother. "Claire should have it," she said. "It belonged to her mother—"

"I insist."

Grandmother Colette's voice was kind yet firm, and even I knew that there would be no arguing with her.

"Thank you for the mirror, Grandmother Colette," I said. "I will treasure it always."

Her smile looked like it could hardly contain all the emotion behind it. "I know that you will, dear girl," she told me.

Then Camille and I bade her good night and left the room. I couldn't wait to get back to my own room and find just the right place to display my mother's mirror. But I knew that there was something important that had to come first.

"Your father's journal," I told Camille. "We've got to go get it. After what happened to Claudia's diary when we left it alone in her room—"

Camille's eyes widened. "You're right!" she exclaimed. "I hadn't thought about it, but if Papa's journal should disappear too . . ."

Camille didn't need to finish her sentence. We both started walking faster. When we reached Claudia's room, I thought, *What if Pierre's journal is gone? It will be all my fault since I gave it to her here. And what if Philippe blames Alexandre for its loss?* I was almost afraid to open the door.

But I did it anyway.

At first glance, the room seemed exactly as we'd left it—wind-up animals scattered by the window, my lamp burning brightly on the writing desk, Pierre's journal sitting in the warm glow it cast. But as I looked closer, I realized that something had, in fact, changed. Pierre's journal was still there—thank goodness for that—but it wasn't alone.

Another book had been carefully placed beside it.

I recognized the burgundy cover at once and thought my heart might explode. Camille grabbed hold of my arm.

"Look," she whispered, pointing. "Isn't that . . . ?"

"Yes," I said. "It's my mother's diary."

9

We both stood completely still for a moment, as if a spell had been cast over us. It seemed so very much like a dream that I was worried any movement or misstep would cause it all to slip away.

But we couldn't spend the rest of our lives standing like statues, so I hurried across the room and scooped up the diary. It was solid in my hands, solid and real and so precious to me, I knew I'd never be able to find the words to express how I felt about it. I tried anyway, though. "Her hands held this book," I whispered. "Her words fill these pages."

"To think it's been returned to you! I don't understand *how*."

"Someone knew," I said thoughtfully, still clinging to the diary as if I'd never let go. "Someone knew we were here, then knew we were gone. But we weren't gone for very long."

"It couldn't have been Madame Colette. She was with us the whole time," Camille said. "But Bernadette—"

"You think Bernadette had the diary?" I asked.

Camille shook her head. "No, actually, I don't," she replied. "I don't think that Bernadette even knows about it. What I meant to say was, if Bernadette knew we were here, then *anyone* could've known we were here."

"So we're still no closer to finding out who took it."

"But that hardly matters now," Camille reminded me gently. "It's been returned to you. At last you can read it!"

"We can both read it," I corrected her. Whatever secrets were written within these pages, I knew that I didn't want to learn them without Camille by my side. We took turns reading the diary entries aloud.

5 July 1898

*Mother and Father say that I cannot keep my baby. It would be a scandal, they say, since my*

marriage to H— was never formally announced
and has been kept secret from everyone we know.
Mother has promised to find my baby a wonderful
family and a wonderful home, where she will be
loved and cared for. But in my heart, I know that I
will never allow it. This is <u>my</u> baby and I will raise
her. No matter what it takes.

10 August 1898

I continue to make arrangements for my little
one's arrival. I have already knit two sweaters for
her and six pairs of booties. They are so impossibly
tiny! How I love to imagine the dear little toes they
will keep warm through the cold winter months
ahead.

I have also made preparations on a grander scale,
a secret that I will confess only to these pages. I
have specially ordered a beautiful perambulator

for my baby! I saw an advertisement in one of
the magazines Mother brought me to help pass
the hours of my confinement, and I knew at once
that I had to have it. It's very elegant, made of
shiny white wicker with a satin pillow and quilt.
It won't be ready until springtime, but that's all
right. Already I find myself dreaming of pushing
this beautiful pram through the gardens, showing
Baby all my favorite spots.

"That's the pram I use for Baby Sophie!" Camille
exclaimed, pointing at the page. "I'm sure of it! It
belonged to *me* when I was a baby! I never dreamed
that Madame Claudia was the one who ordered it!"

A sudden chill ran through me, and I wrapped my
arms around myself. *It would have been my pram. If only
they hadn't sent me away—*

But I didn't want to think about that sort of thing,
so I continued reading the entry.

*I had to enlist the help of my only friend here
to place my order. He manufactured an errand
into town this morning to take my letter and
payment to the post office. He told me that if he
was successful, he'd leave a red handkerchief at the
entrance to the topiary garden to tell me so. Even
now I can see just the tip of it, fluttering slightly in
the breeze.*

Something about those lines felt awfully familiar.

"Wait," I said suddenly, reaching for Pierre's journal. I turned the pages quickly until I reached an entry near the middle. "Listen to this: 'Unexpected trip into town today, but no one is the wiser. A red handkerchief sacrificed to a good cause. Always happy to bring a smile to Little C's face, especially of late.'"

"Do you think that's *my* papa Claudia's writing about?" Camille asked breathlessly. "Do you think that *he* was her only friend?"

"There's no date on your father's journal entry," I told her, "but I don't see any other possible explanation."

"It would make sense, I think," she said thoughtfully, "knowing what we do about his inspiration for the topiary garden. Oh, Claire! I'm so proud of him! To think that he was kind to your mother when she felt so alone in the world!"

I remembered how alone I'd felt when I first arrived at Rousseau Manor and the kindness from Camille that had brightened my very first day here. "It's not a bit surprising to me," I told her. "You two seem very much alike."

I pressed Claudia's journal into Camille's hands. "Here," I said. "You read now."

31 *August* 1898

*Another argument with Mother and Father*
*tonight. They simply won't listen when we talk,*
*so I think I will have no choice but to write them*
*a letter and hope that my words will be more*
*powerful written on the page than when spoken*
*in my voice. It weighs heavily on my heart that we*
*should come to such an impasse—and so soon after*

*I promised myself that I would respect and honor my parents, as is right and fitting. But with every passing day I am more convinced that I will raise this child myself. Under no circumstances will I allow anyone to take her from me.*

*I must not entertain such upsetting thoughts right before bed, so I'll write now of something joyful. I have chosen a name for her! She will be called—*

Suddenly, Camille stopped speaking. She stared at the page as if she could no longer understand what was written there.

"What?" I asked. Oh, how I hoped that Claudia had named me! It would be one more special connection with the mother I'd never known.

But Camille didn't answer.

"What does it say?" I asked impatiently.

Camille took a deep breath, but when she spoke, her voice was hushed. "She will be called Camille."

We stared at each other in silence, unblinking, uncomprehending. I reached over and took the diary from her. Sure enough, there it was, as clear as day in my mother's hand:

*She will be called Camille.*

"I . . . ," I finally said. "I . . . don't understand."

"That's because it doesn't make any sense," Camille said. "I suppose Madame Colette and Monsieur Henri could've ignored Claudia's wishes about what you were supposed to be called. It would've been wrong and terrible, but I suppose it's a possibility."

"Do you think your father and mother let Claudia name you when you were born? Your father loved her so," I suggested. It seemed a very odd sort of thing to do. Surely a mother would want to name her own baby!

*Then again, if Pierre was so kind to Claudia, perhaps his wife was too*, I thought.

"We should—," I started to say, but Camille was already on her feet.

"Come on," she said. "We've got to ask Mama."

I nodded as I closed the diary and tucked it under my arm, along with Pierre's journal. I wasn't going to leave either of them alone, not for a second.

When we reached Marie and Camille's rooms, Marie was still wearing her work dress, though she

117

had taken down her hair. She did not look surprised to see us.

As I closed the door, I opened my mouth to speak, then thought better of it. This was Camille's mother, and it was her question to ask.

"Mama," she began.

A long look passed between them.

"Mama," Camille repeated. "Did you name me? Or was it Madame Claudia who chose my name?"

When Marie didn't answer, Camille continued.

"We were reading Madame Claudia's diary, and she wrote about naming her baby Camille. So now we're confused about why Claire wasn't named Camille but I was."

I held out the diary so that Marie could read the entry herself, but she didn't take it from me. Then, to my surprise, she hid her face in her hands.

*Is she crying?* I wondered. It was hard to tell. I'm sure Camille was thinking the same thing, but she didn't stop speaking.

"So did you name me?"

Camille's question hung there in the air for several seconds. At last Marie lowered her hands. They were trembling a little, but I'm not sure if Camille noticed.

"Come sit by me, dear heart," said Marie.

Camille crossed the room and sat next to her mother.

"The truth is," Marie continued, pressing her hands over Camille's, "that you came to me already named."

"What do you mean?" Camille asked in confusion.

"It was the middle of December, when night falls early. At that time of year, Papa was always home before me, but this particular day the cottage was dark and cold when I entered. I set about to start a fire when the door banged open, and he entered in a rush, a bundle in his arms. . . ."

Marie closed her eyes at the memory, and I found myself leaning forward, hardly daring to imagine what she would say next.

"He said—and I'll never forget it, the way his voice was shaking—he said, 'Sit down, Marie,' and he placed the bundle in my arms. I pulled back a corner of the blanket and saw the most beautiful little face. So small. So peaceful. So perfect. Many questions filled my mind; I hardly knew which to ask first. But before I could say a word, Papa spoke. 'I can answer none of your questions about the babe—not today, not ever,' he said. 'It's a girl, and her name is Camille. Can you love her, Marie? Can you raise her as a daughter and claim her as your own?'"

Camille sat very stiffly, still and quiet; only her eyes moved as she searched Marie's face for the answer.

"And I looked at that baby as I'm looking at you now, and I knew then—as I know now—that I could. That it would be an honor and a privilege to raise you, that the rush of love I felt in that instant would only grow. And it has."

Marie took a deep breath. "So to answer your question: No, I did not name you; nor did I give birth to you. But I give thanks every day for you, Camille. Being your mother is the brightest joy in my life. How lucky I am!"

In a heartbeat, Camille had flung her arms around Marie's neck, and they held each other, crying softly. I felt that I should leave, to give them some privacy, but I was rooted to the spot.

"Papa told you nothing?" Camille asked, her voice muffled. "Not a thing about—where I came from?"

"Not a word, dear heart," Marie said. "I've never wanted to keep secrets from you, but I swore to him that I would never tell you about your adoption. And I knew so very little else."

"I have so many questions and no hope of finding the answers," Camille said. "I don't know if I can bear the mystery of it!"

My heart clenched when I heard those words, for I knew all too well how Camille felt.

Marie looked troubled. "Don't despair, dear girl," she said softly before kissing the top of Camille's head. "Like I always say, the truth will come out in time. The one thing I do know without a doubt is that love surrounds you—wherever you've been, where you are right now, and wherever you shall go."

"I love you, Mama," Camille whispered as she rested her head on Marie's shoulder. Then, I knew, it was long past the time when I should have excused myself. I stood up quietly, not wanting to disturb them, but it was too late.

"Claire," Camille said. "I'm sorry. I was so caught up—"

"There's no need to apologize," I said. "I know this

evening has been ... not at all what we expected." Had it really been just twenty-four hours since my grandparents had broken such shocking news to me?

Camille walked me to the door. Just before we said good night, I took her hand and pulled her into the hallway. "Listen," I whispered in a rush. "There *is* hope of finding the answers. Tomorrow morning, after breakfast, meet me in the parlor."

"I'll be there," she replied. "What do you have planned?"

"I'm not sure yet," I admitted. "But I'll think of something. I promise."

I hurried down the hall as Camille closed the door behind me with a soft *click. Another promise to keep,* I told myself, remembering the vow I'd made to Alexandre about finding a way for him to keep playing the violin. Of course, making a promise was easy. Keeping it—when you didn't have the faintest idea how to do such a thing—was the hard part.

But I would not let them down.

I paused briefly at the door to my room, but I didn't go in. After all, my lamp was still glowing in Claudia's old room, and her diary was still tucked under my arm.

And I had a long night of reading ahead of me.

10

$\mathcal{T}$rue to her word, Camille was waiting in the parlor after breakfast the next morning. She started in surprise when Grandmother Colette and Grandfather Henri entered alongside me. Whatever she had been expecting, it wasn't this.

"Good morning, my little bee," Grandfather Henri said to her. He looked at Camille, then at me, then back to her again, as if trying to figure out why we were all gathered together. Or maybe he already had an idea of what we'd be discussing.

"Good morning," she replied with a curtsy.

"I have the distinct feeling that the girls have been planning something," Grandmother Colette said lightly, but the smile on her face seemed faint and likely to fade.

"We were hoping to speak with you," I said.

Grandfather Henri nodded brusquely. "Your timing

is excellent," he said, "for we have been wanting to speak with you both as well."

When we were all seated, I showed Claudia's diary to my grandparents. "We found Claudia's diary. It was returned to us as mysteriously as it disappeared," I said. "I've had the chance to read it now. So has Camille— parts of it, at least. But there are still things that don't make sense. If I'm Claudia's baby, why wasn't *I* named Camille, the way she wished? And as for Camille—"

"Mama doesn't know where I came from," Camille interrupted me, speaking all in a rush. "Do *you*? Please tell me that you do. Please tell me that Papa didn't take this secret to his grave, or else I shall wonder forevermore—"

Grandmother Colette crossed the room to us at once. "Oh, my dear girls," she said as she took hold of our hands. "Henri, we've made a terrible mess of things, just as we feared we would."

"All that's left to do, then, is make it right," he replied. His voice seemed more gruff than usual, as if he was holding back his emotion.

"Let us speak first, and perhaps we may answer your questions before you can even ask them," Grandmother

Colette said. "There is no easy way to begin. I suppose we should just come out and say it. . . ."

Her voice faltered before trailing off into silence. Grandmother Colette was struggling so much to find the words that for a moment I felt guilty for putting her in such an uncomfortable position. *But we have a right,* I reminded myself. *We have a right to know the truth.*

Grandmother Colette tried again. "Claire, we told you that Claudia died giving birth," she began. "What we should have said—the more accurate answer—is that Claudia died giving birth to twins."

I couldn't breathe.

Twins?

*Twins?*

I had a—a—

No. I couldn't even let myself imagine it, not for a moment. Because if I was mistaken, if I had misheard her, I wouldn't just be embarrassed.

I would be crushed.

"Claire first, then Camille," Grandmother Colette continued. "Twin girls, precious and perfect from the moment you were born."

"Sisters," Grandfather Henri spoke up. "The both of you. Do you understand what we're trying to say?"

I shifted in my seat to look at Camille, seeing her through new eyes. Did we look alike? I hadn't given the matter any thought before, but now—as we stared at each other—it seemed ridiculous that I hadn't noticed sooner. Her hair was longer than mine, and she had more freckles scattered across her pale face, but her eyes—yes, of course, our eyes were a perfect match. Pale green one moment, pale blue the next, shifting colors like the surface of a lake on a windy day. Right now Camille's eyes were wide with wonderment, and I suspected that mine were too. I reached for her hand and squeezed it tightly; she squeezed back in response. *That's what it means to have a sister,* I realized with a jolt. *Someone to sit with you. Someone to take your side. Someone to hold your hand when the truth cracks your world wide open.*

"We couldn't have been more shocked," Grandmother Colette said. "We'd made arrangements for one baby, not two. And then, before we even had a chance to make sense of your arrival, Claudia—"

"She was gone so fast," Grandfather Henri said,

shaking his head as if he still couldn't quite believe it.

"The shock and the grief—neither one of us was strong enough to withstand it," Grandmother Colette said. "We were in no condition to raise one newborn, let alone two. I honestly wasn't sure if I'd ever be able to look upon you without grieving the loss of my daughter all over again." She paused and tried to smile at us. "I know now that I can."

"Cousin Nicolas could take only one of you," Grandfather Henri said. "So we entrusted you to his keeping, Claire, and he and Annabelle were gracious enough to name you in the family tradition."

"The girls on my side of the family have always been given names beginning with the letter *C*," Grandmother Colette explained. Then she turned to Camille. "Pierre LeClerc had worked for us for nearly twenty years. We trusted him completely. He was the only one on the staff who ever even knew that Claudia had been expecting a baby."

"More than that, Claudia trusted him," said Grandfather Henri. "He had always been so kind to her, even when she was a little girl plucking his best blooms to braid a crown of flowers for her hair. I remembered—and I thought—what a fine father he'll make—"

"With a sweet young wife who was already adored by everyone at Rousseau Manor," added Grandmother Colette. "We could never have turned you over to strangers, Camille. Pierre and Marie—well, they were good-hearted and kind and loyal."

"We asked two things of Pierre," Grandfather Henri said. "First, that he tell no one the truth of your parentage. And second, that he name you Camille."

"After all, that was what Claudia wanted," Grandmother Colette said, dabbing at her eyes.

"So you see, Camille, not even Marie knew a thing—until a few days ago," Grandfather Henri said. "She happened to pass by Claudia's room and overheard you two reading the diary and took it. She thought that Claudia must've been your mother, Camille. She came to us and started asking questions. We wanted to tell you both the truth that day, but Marie needed to tell you about your adoption first. That piece of the puzzle needed to come to you from her."

"Mama took the diary?" Camille asked. I was just

as surprised as she was; the thought that Marie had Claudia's diary had never crossed my mind!

"She did," Grandmother Colette said. She stole a glance at Grandfather Henri. "And so now it's all out in the open, and we can move forward with our lives."

Something about what she said—or perhaps the *way* she said it—unsettled me. But before I could figure out why, Camille spoke.

"As long as I can remember, I used to imagine you were ... my grandparents," she said in a small voice. "It feels wrong to say it even now. I used to scold myself for entertaining such a silly dream."

"It wasn't silly, and it wasn't a dream," Grandmother Colette said, placing her hand on Camille's cheek.

"So everything will change now, won't it?" I asked. "Camille is my sister. She is a Rousseau. You can't—she won't—she mustn't be a servant any longer. Not one more day."

"That is our intention," Grandmother Colette said quickly.

"In due time," added Grandfather Henri.

"What do you mean, 'in due time'?" I asked incredulously. "She's your *granddaughter*."

Camille pressed my hand, but I couldn't tell if she meant it as a warning or a thank-you.

"Your reaction does you credit, my dear," Grandmother Colette said. "But it is of the utmost importance that this secret be kept among us. For a little longer, at least."

"You must understand," Grandfather Henri spoke up before I could protest. "It is for your own protection."

My shoulders stiffened. "For our *protection*? Protection from whom?"

"Are we in danger?" asked Camille.

"Not if you keep this secret," replied Grandfather Henri.

Silence followed; I don't think any of us knew what to say.

"Our father—," I began.

"No," Grandmother Colette said. "He is dead and gone, and there is nothing to be said about him."

Grandfather Henri spoke up then. "Claire, I know we are asking a great deal of you. We have only just met, and in this short time you have learned our darkest secrets and most shameful deceptions. You have no reason to trust us—none at all."

"And yet that's what we need you to do now," Grandmother Colette implored me. "Please—if you can find it in your heart—"

With all eyes on me, I squirmed uncomfortably in my seat. I'd set my mind on getting answers today, but they had led to only more questions . . . and more secrets. How could I make this decision? I simply didn't know enough about the situation, about my grandparents, about anything.

And yet there was someone right here—right beside me—who did.

"I leave it up to Camille," I said, turning to my sister. We stared at each other for a long moment.

"If you knew them the way I know them, it would be so much easier," she said. "I trust them. I will keep this secret."

"Then so shall I," I declared. "But it's not right that I should be treated like a pampered daughter of the family while you are a servant, Camille. I don't see how I can abide by it."

"I don't work much like a servant anymore," Camille told me. "I have hardly any tasks. Helping Mama in the kitchen—well, I'll always try to be of use to her, no matter what. And I love caring for Baby Sophie. It's hardly a chore!"

"I told Bernadette and Marie that you were to be relieved of all housework duties once you took it upon yourself to clean the stove that day," Grandmother Colette told her. Then she rose abruptly, on unsteady feet. "I apologize that I must take my leave. The strain—I—I feel a headache coming."

Grandfather Henri rose too, a look of concern on his face. "Let me help you, my love," he said as he took Grandmother Colette's arm.

But before they left the parlor, Grandmother Colette glanced back at us. "Our conversation is not over," she promised. "Merely postponed for another time."

Then they were gone, leaving Camille and me alone. She smiled shyly at me.

"Sisters!" she said, marveling.

"Sisters," I echoed.

"Nothing in the world could make me happier," she said.

"We have so much to discuss," I told her. "I want to know everything about you!"

"And I, you," she said. But a frown settled over her face. "I have to watch Baby Sophie now, though. This afternoon?"

"Yes," I said. "Come to my room whenever you are able."

"I will," she said. "I agree with Madame—I mean Grandmother—Colette. This is only the beginning!"

11

*I* went to my room then, glad for the chance to spend some time alone. Everything I'd learned—everything I'd discovered—had left me feeling scattered and uncertain, like I'd been tossed about on an ocean of secrets, powerless to control my own destiny. I didn't like it—not one bit.

More than anything, I wished that I could turn to Mother and Father to help me make sense of it all. I fastened Mother's cameo to my dress and nestled Father's violin under my chin. Then I tried to figure out where to place my fingers on the strings, but none of the positions seemed right. When I tried moving the bow across the strings, the sound made me shudder.

Dreadful!

I took a long look at myself in the mirror and faced the truth: Playing the violin simply wasn't one of my talents. I didn't even like it that much, and there was nothing wrong with that. After all, what I'd always loved was listening to *Father* play the violin. Not playing it myself. And that's when I figured out how to keep the other promise I'd made.

With a soft piece of wool flannel, I polished the violin one last time. Then I gently returned it to its case. The buckles latched with a satisfying *click*.

I tucked Father's violin under my arm and went outside to the gardens. Alexandre and his father weren't hard to find; they were busy working in the topiary gardens, using sharp clippers to sculpt an enormous elephant. They stopped at once when they saw me.

"Please pardon the interruption," I said. Then I held out the violin case to Alexandre. "This is for you. I want you to have it."

Alexandre and his father stared at me in disbelief.

"I couldn't—," Alexandre began to say, before Philippe interrupted him.

"Mademoiselle Claire, you are too generous for your own good," he said. "Please, take your violin back into the house. Alexandre's place is here, learning a trade by my side. A beautiful instrument like that would be wasted on him."

"It's wasted on me!" I replied. "Alexandre's got real talent. I should know; I grew up listening to my father play. It would be such a shame if Alexandre didn't have the chance to play, considering his passion for it."

I could tell that Philippe was about to object, so I pressed on. "And the truth is, I would consider it a personal favor if you would allow Alexandre to play for me," I told him. "I miss the sound very much. It would remind me of my father to hear his violin played by someone as talented as your son.

"Now, I know that Alexandre has many duties here at Rousseau Manor, and I would hate to infringe on them," I continued. "So, if it's all right with you, I would be happy to help tend the flower garden to allow Alexandre the opportunity to practice his music. Perhaps Camille could help as well."

"You don't have to do that," Alexandre spoke up.

"But I want to," I told him. "My mother took great joy in her gardens, and being with the flowers here—especially the ones she loved so much—makes me feel close to her."

"It doesn't seem right," Philippe said, but even as he said the words, he sounded unsure.

"We can ask my gr—cousins if you wish," I said, "but I assure you they would be more than happy to encourage Alexandre's musical pursuits. Camille has had all sorts of lessons over the years, thanks to their generosity."

Alexandre and I both stared at Philippe hopefully. At last he relented.

"Very well," he said. "Thank you, Mademoiselle Claire."

"Yes, thank you!" Alexandre cried in delight. "It will be my pleasure to play for Camille. And you, of course. Any time at all!"

"Tomorrow morning, perhaps?" I suggested. "If the weather's fine, I'd like nothing more than to spend the day in the flower garden."

"I'll find you there," Alexandre promised. "Oh, and the flowers your mother loved? I learned their name. They're called lilies."

I smiled gratefully at him. "Thank you, Alexandre," I said. "I'll see you tomorrow. Don't forget to bring the violin. And an extra trowel if you've got one!"

I was back in my room later that day when Camille came to visit. She had a basket of buttery, shell-shaped cookies with her, still warm from the oven. "Mama thought we might enjoy a little something sweet," she said.

"Mmm—delicious!" I cried, taking a bite out of one. Then I gestured toward the writing desk. "Claudia's diary is over there," I told Camille. "I stayed up late last night to read it. Now it's your turn."

Camille eyed it warily. "I'm not sure I'm ready for any more shocks so soon," she said.

"There aren't any," I told her. "Most everything else she wrote was about planning for her baby. Babies. Us. Anyway, it's all very sweet and sad. I *wish* I could've known her."

"So do I."

"You know, there was one thing in the diary that surprised me," I said thoughtfully as I flipped to a page near the back of the book. "Take a look at this."

Camille examined the image on the page. It was the one page of the diary that wasn't covered in words; instead, it featured what appeared to be a rubbing of sorts—though a very unusual one, with a pair of swans on it and the initials *C.R.*

"I know that image!" Camille exclaimed. She reached into her apron pocket and pulled out a silvery disc.

"Where did you get that?" I asked.

"I found it in the topiary garden when Alexandre and his father planted a new rosebush by the swans," she explained, placing the coin in my hand. "I've been carrying it with me ever since, for luck."

As I took a closer look, I realized that Camille's coin had the same swans, but different letters: *H.B.* She noticed it at the same time.

"Not the same at all, are they?" she asked. "Though very similar."

"C.R. . . . H.B.," I said, deep in thought. "C.R. . . . C.R. . . ."

"Claudia Rousseau," Camille said suddenly.

"Which would mean H.B. was—"

"Her husband—"

"H— from the diary."

"Our father!"

Our words were like sparks, making our ideas catch fire. Neither one of us could speak fast enough.

"What was his coin doing in the garden?"

"If Claudia had *both* coins, why did she make a rubbing of just the one?"

"You know what this means?" I cried. "Claudia's coin—C.R.—must still be here! Hidden somewhere at Rousseau Manor!"

"We'll check the topiary garden first," Camille declared. "Perhaps Claudia buried them there for safe-keeping, or asked Papa to bury them for her!"

But my mind had already raced ahead to more pressing matters. "It's not just the other coin we've got to find," I said urgently. "It's also our father."

The seriousness of the situation settled over Camille at once. "But . . . he's dead," she said.

"His family, then," I replied. "Don't you see, Camille? When I arrived here, I thought all I had left in the world were a pair of distant cousins I'd never met. And now I have grandparents and a twin sister of my very own! Our father may be gone, but what about *his* parents? We could have another set of grandparents out there somewhere."

"Aunts . . . uncles . . . even cousins!" she exclaimed as her eyes lit up with excitement.

"A whole secret family we know nothing about!" I

cried. "What do you say, Camille? Will you help me search for them?"

"Of course I will," she vowed. "You're my sister. There's nothing I wouldn't do for you. And there's nothing we can't do together."

That was the moment when I realized just how important this undertaking would be. Finding our father's family would be more than a challenge; it was a chance. A chance to set things right after so many years of being wrong. Secrets, as I had learned too well, could shatter families.

But the truth?

The truth could make them whole.

If you like Secrets of the Manor,
then check out this other great series,

# sew zoey!

Read on for a sneak peek at

sew zoey

READY TO WEAR

by Chloe Taylor

# CHAPTER 1

*Creeeak...*

*Thud!*

Zoey Webber heard the glamorous thump of glossy paper meeting floorboards, and raced down the hall to the front door to get the mail. Only one thing could make that sound: the newest issue of

*Très Chic* arriving through the mail slot.

*Yes!*

She scooped it up along with some envelopes and interior design magazines and put everything but *Très Chic* on a table for her aunt. Then she scanned the cover to see what was *très chic* for July:

**The Long (Dresses) and Short (Shorts) of Summer Style**

**Dots Are Hot!**

**25 Fresh Fashion Faces to Watch**

**Be Inspired . . . by BOLD Colors!**

Zoey grinned at the last headline. Oh, she *was* inspired.

She was also lucky. She was spending her summer days at Aunt Lulu's house instead of the usual: being stuck at home with her big brother, Marcus, as her babysitter, or stuck at day camp for what felt like the hundredth year in a row. This summer was different. Her brother was busy with a part-time job and her dad finally agreed that she was getting a little old for day camp . . . at least if she didn't want to go.

Zoey discovered pretty quickly that "Aunt Lulu camp" was better than any day camp. Aunt Lulu ran her interior design business out of her home office, but even when she had to work, she made it fun for Zoey. She let Zoey suggest fabrics and color combinations for clients' inspiration boards and make collages and paper doll clothes with old wallpaper samples. And if she had to go out for a meeting or something, she actually *paid* Zoey to dog-sit—which basically meant watching Aunt Lulu's fourteen-year-old mutt, Draper, snore.

Plus, Zoey and her aunt loved doing a lot of the same things: getting mani-pedis, baking cookies, reading magazines, watching old movies, and indulging in reality TV shows—they both were hands-down obsessed with fashion design competitions. Too bad Dad and Marcus couldn't stand them. "Boys will be boys," Aunt Lulu always said.

Zoey walked over to the kitchen table without taking her eyes off the magazine cover for a second. She sat down on a chair and then gently let the magazine's uncracked spine fall open to a random page. It landed on a perfume sample. It was the newest in a popular line of scents by a young fashion designer. Zoey closed her eyes and took a whiff, inhaling the amber and tuberose, and letting her mind wander. . . .

*What if I were a fashion designer someday?* she imagined. *I'd get to look at pretty clothes and read magazines all day long! Maybe I'd make my own perfume too, and it would smell like . . . um . . . gardenias? Yeah. And maybe one day I'd be in* Très Chic's *"Day in the Life of a Designer" section! How cool would that be if it really happened?*

It might have just been a daydream, but it sounded pretty amazing to Zoey. She sighed, put the magazine down on the table, and began to flip through the pages, scanning each spread to make sure she saw every square inch of it.

*Beep-beep.*

Zoey quickly lifted her head. Did she hear a beeping sound?

Yep, that was definitely her phone saying a text had just come in!

"Coming!" she yelled toward the muffled ringtone. She stood up and looked around the kitchen.

*Beep-beep.*

She twirled in place. Where exactly *was* her phone? She was sure she'd left it on the table . . . but it wasn't there.

Maybe on the kitchen counter? Nope. She even checked inside the fridge.

She crawled around under the table in case it had dropped on the floor. Still no luck!

"Excuse me, Draper," she said as she gently slid her hand under his belly. Maybe he fell asleep on top of her phone? His ear twitched and his leg kicked, but his snoring never stopped. She groaned and started to get up.

*Beep-beep.*

Okay . . . her phone had to be somewhere . . . somewhere very close. She had spent most of the morning planted at the kitchen table drawing imaginary outfits in her newest sketchbook. It was her favorite thing to do at Camp Lulu by far.

At the beginning of summer, Aunt Lulu noticed all the fashion drawings Zoey was doing on the back of used printer paper and started hanging them on the fridge.

When there was no space left in the "art gallery," as Aunt Lulu started to call it, she surprised Zoey with a beautiful sketchbook tied with a big raffia bow. "I'm glad you're saving the Earth, but drawings like yours deserve to be on something better than scrap paper, don't you think?" she had asked. "Plus, I don't want you to lose any of them!"

And the rest, as they say, was history—soon Zoey had filled a few sketchbooks with original clothing designs. Well, some were inspired by her favorite designers, like Blake and Bauer and the amazing Daphne Shaw, especially in the beginning. But most of them were unique, and her aunt loved them all. She loved the silly ones, like the "sunny day sundress" made of sky-blue fabric dotted with puffy white clouds. And she even loved the unwearable ones, like the flapper dress made entirely of those plastic rings that hold together six-packs of soda cans. Zoey didn't show the sketchbooks to anyone else. Not even to her best friends, Priti and Kate. She just did it for fun . . . and because once she got started, she couldn't stop coming up with ideas.

It was pretty funny, actually, that she spent so

much time dreaming up different outfits. During the school year, she had to wear the same exact thing every single day: five days a week of a standard-issue school uniform. Sometimes she wondered if she would be so obsessed with clothes if she actually got to wear them!

But right now she had a much more vital question on her mind: Where on earth was her phone?

Wait . . . her sketchbook was looking awfully thick.

She flipped through the pages . . . and *there* it was! On top of a drawing of a floor-skimming maxi dress and a scallop-edged white tank paired with geometric-print pedal pushers.

She laughed, breathed a sigh of relief, and looked down at the screen to see who was sending all those texts.

**Can you believe it?!** said the first text. Then there was a: **Hello??** Finally came an: **Um, Zoey? R u there?**

The text messages were from Priti Holbrooke, one of Zoey's two very best friends.

Zoey picked up her phone and gawked at the screen as a million thoughts flew through her head.

Believe *what*? She had no idea!

And was it good? (She hoped!)

Or bad . . . (Uh-oh!)

*Priti!* Zoey loved her because she knew how to make life more exciting. But sometimes she could give you a heart attack!

Zoey thumbed back a speedy, desperate reply: **Believe what?!?!**

She clutched her phone and waited, staring at the screen. . . .

Still, she jumped when it beeped and blinked to life again.

**No more uniforms!** texted Priti.

Zoey's mouth fell open and she nearly dropped the phone. "No way!" she cried out loud, reading it over again to be sure.

Could it be that after sixty-five years, Mapleton Prep was finally waking up? Could it be that the petition Zoey started last spring had actually worked? She started it because she didn't feel like everyone else, and she didn't want to *dress* like everyone else, either. But she never thought it would work.

The school wasn't really that bad overall. The

classrooms had big windows. Most of the teachers were nice. And except for the gelatinous meat loaf and cardboard pizza, the food was mostly edible. It was just those uniforms! All that horrible gray polyester. And those plaid ties. Every time Zoey got dressed for school in them, she could swear a part of her soul died.

**R u sure?** she texted back.

**Yes! +!!!!!!!!** came the answer right away.

Zoey did a little dance of joy and quickly pressed call instead of reply.

"Hi!" answered Priti.

"How did you find out? Are you sure?" Zoey blurted.

"Zoey, we got a letter in the mail!" Priti told her. "Haven't you seen it? It came today!"

Zoey groaned. "Ugh, I missed it! I'm at my aunt's house. What does it say?"

"Hang on." Zoey could hear Priti moving around and shuffling some papers. "It's here somewhere . . . *Tara!*" Priti hollered to one of her sisters as Zoey pulled the phone away from her ear. "Where's the mail? I need that letter from my school!"

While she waited, Zoey could picture the likely scene taking place in the Holbrooke home. There was always a lot going on with three girls as lively as Priti and the twins. Tara and Sashi were in high school, and each had their own *niche*, as their dad liked to say. Sashi played the piano . . . and the flute and the harp, and sang, too. Her primary goal in life these days was earning a scholarship to Juilliard. Tara, on the other hand, was all about biology and organic chemistry and basically anything that screamed pre-med. She was spending the summer working in a college lab.

Priti was the baby of the family and the opposite of her focused, organized older sisters. Her grades were fine and her work was never late. And yet her bedroom and her backpack might as well have been black holes. She wasn't exactly a slob . . . but maybe she was, a little bit. Whatever she lacked in organizational skills, however, she more than made up for in overall spunk and charm. Zoey could always count on Priti to cheer her up if she was feeling down. Or to make her laugh until her stomach hurt.

"Sorry about that, Zoey," Priti said. "Zoey? Are you still there?"

"Yes!" Zoey answered. "Read it to me! Hurry! Who's the letter from?"

"Our new principal," Priti told her. "Her name is Ms. Austen. Ms. *Esther* Austen . . . Esther? What a name, right? Anyway, 'Dear Students and Families,' she says, 'I hope this letter finds you well and that you are enjoying your summer' . . . blah, blah, blah, you get the idea."

"*Yes!*" Zoey said, tapping her fingers on the table.

"Okay . . . 'As well as introducing myself, I'm writing to announce some exciting changes at Mapleton Preparatory. First, we will be expanding the music department—'"

"*Music department!*" Zoey groaned. "Priti. You're killing me. Get to the uniform part, please!"

"Patience, patience," Priti teased her. "Just kidding. Here it is . . . 'And finally, after extensive thought and debate, we will no longer be requiring students to wear uniforms.'" She paused and waited for Zoey's reaction. "Zoey? Are you there? Did you faint or something?"

# Did you LOVE reading this book?

Visit the Whyville...

## Where you can:

- Discover great books!
- Meet new friends!
- Read exclusive sneak peeks and more!

Log on to visit now!
bookhive.whyville.net

# sewzoey

If you love the gorgeous gowns
in Secrets of the Manor,
wait until you meet Zoey Webber,
a seventh-grade fashion designer!
Check out the Sew Zoey books,
available at your favorite store!